400 FIRST KISSES

E. L. TODD

This is a work of fiction. All the characters and events portrayed in this novel are fictitious or used fictitiously. All rights reserved. No part of this book may be reproduced in any form or by any electronic or mechanical means, including information storage and retrieval systems, without written permission from the publisher or author, except in the case of a reviewer, who may quote brief passages in a review.

Hartwick Publishing

400 First Kisses

Copyright © 2017 by E. L. Todd

All Rights Reserved

PROLOGUE

BREE

I took the stairs to the third floor with the phone placed against my ear. "Amelia, everything is ready to go, right?"

My sister shushed everyone in the background so she could hear me talk. "Everyone is here. Evan is running a little late, but he said he's pulling into the parking lot. I've got the balloons and the cake. We're ready to go, lady."

"Perfect." I walked down the hall and approached Cypress's apartment. I was throwing him a surprise birthday party, a mixture of my friends and his. "I'm almost there. I'll give him my birthday present then offer to take him out to dinner. He'll have no idea. It's gonna be awesome."

"I can't believe you went to this much trouble for him. You've only been dating for three months." Amelia had always been the responsible one, paying every bill early because even on time was too late. She liked to live life by the book, following every rule like it was one of the ten commandments. Sometimes it annoyed me, but she always meant well. Besides, she was my sister. I had to like her, even during the times when I didn't.

"Well, you know I fell in love with him on our first date." I met Cypress in college. We had business law together, but we didn't start dating until after graduation. He had a girlfriend at the time, but luckily, that didn't last long. Once I finally had him, I knew I wasn't going to let him go. It was one of the rare moments in my life when I just knew it was going to work out.

I approached his door then lowered my voice. "Alright, I gotta go."

"See ya soon."

I hung up and shoved my phone into my back pocket. He had given me a copy of his key recently, so I dug in my purse until I found it. I unlocked the door then stepped inside. I was just about to open my mouth and call for him when I heard something I didn't like.

"Cypress…"

I stilled in the entryway, feeling the dread sink in my stomach like a brick. My pulse pounded in my ears, and adrenaline spiked in my blood. My lungs worked hard to get enough air to my brain, but the rest of my body didn't want to cooperate.

When I turned toward his bedroom, I saw a case of beer sitting on the table with a pink bow on top. The bed squeaked as two heavy bodies worked together. Even though I knew exactly what I was going to see, I walked toward the open doorway and saw a scene I'd never forget as long as I lived.

Cypress lay on his back while his ex-girlfriend rode him like a cowgirl.

His hands gripped her hips and guided her up and

down, his eyes homed in on her shaking tits. He didn't even notice me in the doorway.

My initial reaction was to cry then run.

But I wasn't going to do either of those things.

I grabbed the case of beer she must have brought and popped the cap off a few with the bottle opener I kept on my keyring. Foam poured over and spilled on my hands, but I couldn't care less about the stickiness.

I stormed into the bedroom with three bottles in each hand then turned them upside down, spilling hot beer and foam all over their bodies.

"What the hell?" She covered her hair, as if that would do anything to stop the beer from soaking into her strands.

Cypress locked eyes with me, and his guilt outweighed the beer that was currently soaking into his mattress and ruining his belongings. When he opened his mouth to speak, I poured more beer right over the opening so he choked on his own words.

"Asshole." I threw the empty bottles on the ground, listening to them shatter as I walked off with my head held high. There was no way in hell I was gonna shed a tear in front of a guy who didn't deserve it. No way in hell was I gonna let his whore know she hit me where it hurt. I opened the front door and made sure I had the last word before I left. "Happy birthday."

1

Bree

My Spanish windows were wide open, and the sound of the mourning doves reached my ears. With a slow coo, they made their hypnotic noises and slowly pulled me away from my dreams and into reality. When I was fully awake, I purposely kept my eyes closed so I could enjoy the serenity for just a moment longer.

Carmel was the most peaceful place in California. The weather was always forgiving and moderate, and the small population of four thousand people made it easy to walk everywhere in town. I couldn't remember the last time I drove anywhere.

I pulled the sheets higher over my shoulders and listened to the ocean in the background. I lived on Casanova and 7th, four streets from the water. Early in the morning and late in the evening, it was quiet enough that I could hear the waves and the seagulls. Some people fell asleep to the sound of their TV. I fell asleep to the sound of the nature around me.

When I couldn't stay in bed any longer because my

full bladder was aching for release, I finally got up and went to the bathroom. The windows were open in there as well, so I listened to the doves everywhere I went. The sun was already out that morning, and there was a hint of a breeze.

It was going to be a beautiful day.

I walked downstairs and rubbed the sleep from my eyes. I needed to make some coffee in my French press before I could become fully awake and able to get to work. I needed to get down to the Hippopotamus Café, the restaurant I owned on Ocean Avenue, to do the books and help out with orders.

My grandmother had lived in this house for over thirty years. When she passed away, she willed it to me. It was the only reason I could afford to live here to begin with. Otherwise, I wouldn't have had the money to open up my business.

I made a cup of coffee then walked into the living room. The shades were all pulled down, so I opened each one and took a look outside. The street was quiet, but that wouldn't last long. The locals would be out to enjoy the good weather with their furry dogs in a matter of minutes.

I was just about to turn away from the window when I noticed the neighboring house on the left. Last time I'd checked, the house was still for sale as it had been for over a year. Apparently, someone must have bought it because the for sale sign was gone and the windows were wide open. A truck was parked in the driveway, and the flowers had been newly planted.

Maybe I had new neighbors.

At the end of my driveway sat a few packages I ordered from Amazon. They must have come last night when I was working late. In my black leggings and t-shirt, I walked outside to grab my stuff.

That's when my new neighbor stepped outside. Packages had been placed at the edge of his driveway as well, so that must have been where he was going. Wearing black running shorts and a gray t-shirt, he looked muscular and lean. He filled out every inch of the fabric and was nothing but pure man. Unlike the rest of the residents of my neighborhood, he was young—my age.

I reached the end of my driveway and tried to get a good look at him without making it obvious. But it wasn't out of line for me to introduce myself since we were now neighbors. Nothing wrong with being friendly...and maybe a little more than just friendly. "Are you my new neighbor?"

He reached the last stone step and turned to me, a gorgeous face with a perfectly structured jawline. His eyes were blue like the water, but that prettiness contrasted against his masculinity in every other respect. Strong, sexy, and stud-like, he was gorgeous.

But I already knew him.

Cypress.

I stilled when I recognized his features, the man who broke my heart. He made me fall in love with him, and then he betrayed me, hooking up with his ex when she stopped by to say happy birthday. I'd pretended it hadn't bothered me as much as it really did. Only Amelia and my other friends knew how badly it messed me up.

He didn't seem surprised to see me next door. He walked toward me, even more handsome up close than he was from his driveway. "Morning."

A million different forms of rage shot through my body. The last time I saw Cypress was outside my apartment. He'd apologized and said it was a stupid mistake and he would never do it again, but I'd slammed my door in his face and told him to drop dead.

And now he was my goddamn neighbor.

What the hell?

"Morning?" I blurted. "That's all you have to say? When did you move in?"

"A few days ago." He crossed his arms over his chest, his biceps looking even nicer in the t-shirt.

"I didn't see a moving truck."

He shrugged. "Maybe you weren't paying attention."

"I think I would notice if someone was moving in next door to me." I worked a lot, but I spent the rest of my time at home. I had so many windows that I could see in every direction in my neighborhood. Plus, it was a small town. Nothing went on that we didn't know about.

"Maybe you should get your eyes checked, then." He smiled, like he found this conversation amusing.

"Is this some kind of joke?" I hadn't seen Cypress since we broke up a year ago. Now he'd just showed up next door to me like everything was normal. "If it is, it's not funny."

"Do you see me laughing?" He didn't drop his smile, getting an obvious kick out of this. "You look nice today, by the way."

My hair was thrown in a bun, and I hadn't even brushed my teeth. "Now that was a joke."

"Still not laughing." He stepped around me and walked to the boxes. "You need help with these?"

"I can carry my own—"

He picked everything up anyway and carried it to the front door.

Seriously, what was going on? I followed behind him.

"I don't want you to live next door."

"That's too bad." He opened the front door and invited himself inside. "I was hoping you could water my plants when I'm gone." He set everything on the counter, making himself at home like it wasn't the first time he'd been inside.

"This isn't a joke, Cypress. Did you move next door on purpose?"

He turned around without answering the question. "You want to go on a hike in Point Lobos today? It's gonna be beautiful."

My jaw dropped because I couldn't make sense of any of this. "I have no idea what's going on right now. I hate you. Remember?"

"You don't hate me," he said with that smug grin. "You just *think* you hate me."

"No, I'm pretty sure I hate cheating assholes."

It was the only time in the conversation when his smile faltered.

I walked back to the front door, which was still wide open. "Now, please get out."

"Just trying to be a helpful neighbor." Without further argument, he walked back outside again. "Let me know if you change your mind about Point Lobos."

My eyes snapped wide, and I slammed the door behind him. "What an asshole."

I SHUT ALL MY WINDOWS SO I DIDN'T HAVE TO LOOK AT HIS house next to mine—and more importantly—look into mine. I grabbed my phone and called the first person who came to mind. "Amelia?"

"What's up?" She spoke with a sigh, like she was tired or in the middle of something.

"Can you talk?"

"Yeah. I'm fine. What's up?"

"You won't believe who my next-door neighbor is."

She didn't venture a guess or seem interested in finding out who. "Who?" She was clearly doing something in the background, probably taking care of Rose and Lily, my two little nieces. Rose was four and Lily was two.

"Cypress. I woke up this morning and saw him walk out of the house."

"Wow…strange."

That's all she had to say? "We broke up a year ago, and now he's living next door. I mean, isn't that the strangest thing you've ever heard?"

"It's pretty weird," she said. "But don't worry about it."

Don't worry about it? "Amelia, why do you sound weird? Everything okay."

"I'm just tired. Rose didn't sleep well last night, and I didn't either."

"That's too bad. You need me to help out? Is Evan working today?" I couldn't remember what day of the week it was, actually. I just knew it wasn't the weekend.

"No…" Her voice faltered. "No, I'm okay. But I should get going. Lily is about to eat a bug off the floor."

I still thought it was weird that my sister didn't seem more alarmed by Cypress's sudden appearance, but I didn't push her on it. Maybe she and Evan were having problems. I'd never thought they went well together in the first place. "I'll talk to you later. Love you."

She inhaled a deep breath and went quiet. After several seconds, she finally responded. "I love you too…"

2

Bree

When I woke up, it was a cloudy day. I preferred the sun, but overcast weather didn't usually last past morning. The fog drifted away, and the skies cleared up, revealing the beautiful, beaming sun as it poured across Carmel.

I left the windows open as I went downstairs and made a cup of coffee with my French press. I needed to head to the post office to check the mail and do a few other errands, so I finished my mug and quickly got ready before I left the house.

The house next door had been for sale for nearly a year, but now all the windows were open, and the garden was blossoming with well-groomed flowers. Even a new coat of paint had been added. I wasn't sure who the new neighbor was, but I'd probably bump into them eventually.

I walked up 7th Street and made a left on Dolores. It was uphill most of the way, but I enjoyed the exercise. I managed to keep my weight down because I walked everywhere I needed to go but still got to eat the amazing food all the restaurants provided. I walked past the large windows of La Bicyclette, seeing a couple in the window enjoy their breakfast of poached eggs and fresh baguettes. My stomach rumbled, but I knew it was best to eat at home. I crossed Ocean Street then made a right when I reached the post office. I loved living in Carmel, but I hated not having a physical address to receive mail. I had to check the PO box every other day, not that I minded having another reason to walk somewhere.

The metallic surface of the boxes gleamed with cleanliness, but I knew if they weren't taken care of on a regular basis, they would rust. I found my box in the corner and spun the dial left and right, cracking the code to get my box open.

A man came up right beside me, his PO box directly next to mine. I didn't get a good look at him because we were so close together, but I noticed his arms. They were tight with muscle and corded with veins. His hands were big and muscular, perfect for handling tools, or better yet, a woman. His scent washed over me, and it was innately familiar but unrecognizable.

I pulled out my mail, but I didn't pay attention to what I was doing and dropped a few envelopes on the ground.

He kneeled down and picked them up.

"Thank you."

He stood upright and finally exposed his face, handsome features I'd seen before. "No problem."

I was looking into the face of the man who broke my heart. It couldn't be possible, but no matter how many times I blinked, it was him. He had the same strong jaw, beautiful eyes, and the same hint of arrogance that followed him everywhere he went. "Cypress...?" It was a stupid question to ask because I knew it was him.

"Yours truly." He smiled then unlocked his box. "Haven't checked the mail in a while. Probably all bills... and I hate bills." He tucked everything under his arm and shut the door. "Did you get anything good?"

Why would I care about the mail when my ex-boyfriend was standing next to me? "What's going on?"

"What do you mean?" He leaned against the wall. He wore a long-sleeve t-shirt and dark jeans. Black Keds were on his feet.

I glanced at his PO box before I turned my gaze back to him. "You aren't my new neighbor, are you?"

"Guilty." When he smiled, his eyes lit up in the same sexy way as before. "If you ever need a handyman, you know who to call."

"But...what?" This still wasn't adding up. "Did you move next door to me on purpose?"

"No. It was just a great coincidence."

More like a terrible coincidence. My house was so peaceful. I didn't want to wake up every morning and see the man who broke my heart next door. That sounded like a nightmare, actually. "I don't think our being neighbors is such a good idea." I shut the door and walked away from him, needing a minute of space before I could really accept this. When I woke up that morning, everything felt normal. Now my world had been turned upside down.

He followed me outside, and we walked down Dolores toward 7th. It was still early in the morning, so only the locals were outside. When the tourists arrived around lunchtime, the sidewalk would be packed on either side of Ocean. "I think it's a great idea. We can start our own neighborhood watch."

"There's no crime around here." I read in the *Pine Cone*

that they gave a woman a fine for dropping a donut on the ground. The cops in town didn't have enough to do.

"You can never be too safe, right?" With his long legs, he kept up my pace easily. We passed two women on the sidewalk, and they both looked at him, appreciating his rugged good looks. He hadn't shaved yet, so a thick shadow was covering his chin. His dark brown hair was cut short toward the scalp.

"You're right. I feel a lot safer without you around."

"Come on," he said. "It must feel good to have a strong man right next door. If you ever get scared in the middle of the night, you know who to call."

He had a lot of nerve. "That was ballsy."

He shrugged. "I know what I have to offer."

"When did you become so arrogant?"

"When?" he asked. "I've always been this way."

"Not how I remember it. You were pretty pleasant until you screwed what's-her-name."

Cypress dropped his smile and placed his hands in his pockets. "It was a stupid mistake, and I'll regret that for the rest of my life. She wasn't worth everything I lost."

"Then you shouldn't have done it. It's not that hard not to cheat. People do it every day."

"I was an asshole. I admit it. But I'm different now."

"You're right," I countered. "You're a lot more arrogant than you were a year ago." I walked faster, trying to put some space between us. We passed Conway of Asia, and the owner's bright blue parrot sat in the tree and had his breakfast in a bowl that sat on a branch. Families stopped to see the beautiful bird, but I passed right by, even though I would normally stop and feed him a nut.

"But I'm also more handsome, right?" he asked, his grin returning.

"You look the same to me." Even if he was drop-dead gorgeous, I wouldn't admit it, not after everything he put me through. He sent me into a three-month depression that involved enough tears to severely dehydrate me.

"So you still think I'm hot?"

I rolled my eyes and didn't answer. When we got to 7th, I turned right and walked down the hill.

Cypress finally went quiet and walked beside me in silence. The clouds were already breaking up, and the sun was starting to peek through. We passed a small hotel then the other residences before we arrived at Casanova.

I took a moment to grasp what was happening. The only man I'd ever loved was now my neighbor. And he was also my cheating ex-boyfriend who broke my heart. I wasn't sure how he even knew where I lived.

When we approached our houses, I was relieved we could finally go our separate ways. Without saying goodbye to him, I walked up to my two-story Spanish house and prepared to go inside.

But he was right behind me. "You want to get dinner tonight?"

I turned around. "Are you joking?"

"Not at all. Let's catch up."

Did he think we were friends? "Cypress, I'm not trying to be rude, but I really don't want anything to do with you. I've put everything in the past, but that doesn't mean we need to spend time together just because we're neighbors."

"It's one meal, sweetheart. Even free food doesn't interest you?"

"I can pay for my own meals." Always had and always would.

"I'll pick you up at seven." He walked down my stone steps and headed toward his house.

"Cypress, I said no."

"And I said I'm picking you up at seven. I suggest you be ready." He pulled his mail from under his arm and walked inside his house.

I rolled my eyes and walked inside my own house so I could call Amelia.

Right at seven, he knocked on the door.

I couldn't believe he actually thought we were doing this. I didn't owe him a damn thing. I was the one who threw him a surprise birthday party while he screwed his ex. Before I even opened the door, I was livid. I'd turned down his dinner invitation, and I would do it again. I opened the door and was about to yell at him when I saw a bag of takeout in his hand along with a bottle of wine.

"I knew it would be impossible to get you out of the house, so I brought dinner to us." As if he was welcome in my home, he walked inside and set the food on the mahogany dining table. He pulled out the white takeout boxes then retrieved two wineglasses from the cabinet—knowing exactly where they were. He poured the wine then took a seat.

"Again, you're ballsy."

He opened my white container. "I got you chicken kebabs. I'm sure you'll like it."

"Actually, it's my favorite…" I sauntered to the table and watched him eat as if this interaction were completely normal.

He patted the table with his fingers. "Come on, sweetheart. The food is on the table, and the wine is open. Eat with me. If you say no, I'm still gonna sit here until I'm done. May as well make the best out of it."

I pulled the chair out then sat down. I hadn't eaten anything all day, so I was definitely starving. I sipped the Syrah and loved how dry it was. "This is good."

"I know a little bit about wine."

I grabbed my plastic fork and knife and ate, my head down so I wouldn't have to make direct eye contact with him. If you'd told me yesterday I'd be having dinner with my ex, I wouldn't have believed you. But now he was my neighbor, and I'd have to see him every day.

"How's the café doing?"

I just scooped the rice onto my fork. "How did you know I owned it?"

He shrugged. "People talk."

"It's doing well. Busy as ever."

"That's awesome," he said. "I've eaten there a few times. I really like it."

"Thanks…" I really liked it too. I always thought work was supposed to be a burden, but I enjoyed walking into my restaurant every day. "What do you do?"

"I own a few restaurants too."

"You do?" I had no idea. But that explained why he moved here.

"Yeah. I really enjoy it. There's no place like Carmel. Business here is great."

"I guess we have something in common…" He majored in business just the way I did, but he never told me what he wanted to do with his degree. "Are you seeing someone?" It was an awkward thing to ask, but it was bound to come up. Since he hooked up with Vanessa, I assumed he was seeing her.

"No. I'm totally available." He winked at me.

I rolled my eyes in response. "You aren't my type."

"Really?" he asked with a laugh. "Handsome, smart, wealthy...none of those are on your list?"

"Cheating isn't."

He took a bite of his food and averted his gaze.

I felt bad for rubbing what he did in his face, but he was the one making me spend the evening with him. "I'm seeing someone."

"Oh yeah? Who is he?"

I totally made that up. I just wanted Cypress to leave me alone. If he thought I wasn't available, he might give up. I couldn't think of any reason why he was trying to spend time with me unless he wanted to get back together. Maybe he dated Vanessa for a while and realized what we had was pretty great—until he threw it away. "He works in Monterey...finance guy." Couldn't think of anything better on the spot.

"What's his name?"

"Bradley," I blurted.

"Bradley what?"

"Bradley...Cooper."

He raised an eyebrow, and a wide grin stretched across his face. "*The* Bradley Cooper?"

God, why did I say that? I shouldn't have blurted out the first name that came to mind. "No, not the actor. But he has the same name."

"Uh-huh..."

"I'm serious."

He laughed. "You're such a bad liar. Don't worry, it's cute."

"Well, I'm sorry I'm not a very good liar. Not like you, anyway."

He looked down again and took another bite.

I wasn't sure what was wrong with me. I felt bad for insulting him even though I'd walked in on him screwing his ex-girlfriend. I shouldn't feel bad about anything…but I did.

"I wouldn't care if you had a boyfriend. I'd still like to buy you dinner."

Maybe it was just because he was unbelievably handsome, but those words sank into me, affecting every organ in my body and giving me a slight high. When I'd told him I loved him, I really meant it. Maybe when you loved someone, you always loved them.

"And I'd still like to apologize for what I did. You'll never understand how much that day haunts me. I'd give everything I have for a redo…you have no idea." He touched the wine stem between his fingertips and stared at the red liquid inside.

I didn't have any reason to believe him, but I did. "I accept your apology, Cypress." I never accepted it when he tried to win me back, but I accepted it now. I would never date him again or even be friends with him, but I could at least give him that.

"Thanks." He took a drink then set the glass on the table again. "How do you like your food?"

"It's incredible…like always."

"It's a good place, huh?"

"One of my favorites." He smiled then closed the lid to his container. "Have any plans for the rest of the evening?"

"Watch TV and go to bed."

"That sounds exciting."

"Don't make fun of me. You already know I'm a homebody."

"Yeah…" He smiled. "I remember."

When I was finished, I cleared all the packaging away and wiped down the table. Spending the evening with him wasn't so bad, but I didn't want him to stick around. He couldn't erase the way he hurt me. That trust was broken forever.

Cypress rose from the table, looking appetizing when he stood at his full height. He was the most handsome man I'd ever been with, sexy and mysterious at the same time. I'd be lying if I said I hadn't thought about him once or twice in a sexual way since we'd broken up. But no matter how attractive he was, it didn't fix the scars over my heart.

When the intensity settled on my shoulders and he looked at me like that, I wanted to avoid the situation. I'd been the recipient of that gaze before, and I knew what followed afterward. "Thanks for dinner…" I walked across the hardwood floor and got the door open, feeling the cool night air enter the house once there was a crack in the doorway.

He came up behind me. "My pleasure." He grabbed the door and pushed it shut, making his intentions very clear.

I took a deep breath.

His large hands moved to my waist, and he maneuvered me against the door. His chest was pressed to mine instantly, and his cologne swept over me. His hand slid into my hair just the way I liked, and his soft lips found mine.

He kissed me good.

He kissed me with passion and longing. He kissed me like I was the only woman in the world. His cock was hard in his jeans and pressed right against my hip, just as thick and long as it used to be. He wanted more—undeniably.

I had no idea why I let the kiss go on. My hands moved to his arms, but I never pushed him away. My lips danced with his, and I even gave him my tongue, escalating the kiss when it was already intense. My body produced the same chemical reaction as when we were together before, turning white-hot and burning with arousal. Despite how much he'd hurt me, my body desired his carnally. The chemistry was undeniable. I'd noticed it the first time we were ever close to one another.

But kissing would lead to something more serious, and I couldn't let that happen. I turned my face to the side and scooted away from him, feeling disappointed once the affection ended. I hadn't been with anyone else since we broke up. I dated here and there, but I never had a connection with anyone.

Cypress didn't pressure me again. He stepped away, but he wiped his thumb over the corner of his mouth, his disappointment obvious. His shoulders were tight, and he released a sigh under his breath.

I waited for him to apologize.

But he never did.

He moved both of his hands into his pockets as he stared at me. Instead of walking out the door, he remained still, as if he had more to say.

Now I was just embarrassed and wanted him to leave. "I'm not a hookup, Cypress. And I'll never be one."

"Wasn't looking for a hookup."

"Well, I'll never be with you again either. So, let's just forget that happened and move on."

"We can try to forget about it." He opened the door but didn't walk out. "But we both know it'll be all we can think about."

3

AMELIA

"Rose, did you take my phone?" I eyed my daughter sitting on the couch, her blonde hair already as thick as mine, which was insane for a seven-year-old.

Her feet didn't touch the ground when she sat on the couch. The page of her coloring book was only halfway completed, so something obviously must have sidetracked her. She was meticulous about her projects, reminding me of myself. Thank god she didn't resemble that piece of shit ex-husband of mine. "No…"

Lily screamed from the other couch, tears running down her face as she gripped her arm. She had just gotten stung by a bee, and the poor girl was allergic.

"Rose." My nostrils flared, and I was about to spank her ass. "I need my phone. Your sister needs to see a doctor."

"Then why can't I come?" she cried.

"Rose, I'm not kidding. Give me the phone, or I'm taking away every single toy you have for a whole week." I wasn't messing around now.

She finally hopped off the couch, disappeared down the hallway, and returned with the cell phone.

I was still going to punish her for taking it in the first place. I snatched it out of her hand and called my lifeline.

Cypress answered immediately. "Hey, Amelia. How's it going?"

Lily screamed again.

"That answered my question," he said with a chuckle. "Do you need anything?"

"I know it's your day off, and I'm sorry to bother you—"

"You never bother me," he said seriously. "And you know that."

Cypress was the sweetest guy on the planet. He'd been there for me through everything, my divorce, raising two kids on my own...everything. Without him, I wouldn't have been able to get by. Normally, I had Bree to lean on...but she couldn't do much anymore. "I need to take Lily to urgent care. She got stung by a bee."

"She's allergic, isn't she?" he said. "She just needs an antihistamine, and she'll be okay."

"I still want to take her in to get checked out."

"Okay." He didn't argue. "You need me to watch Rose?"

"Please."

"I'm leaving now. Give me two minutes."

"Thank you so much, Cypress…" There weren't enough words in the English language to explain how much I appreciated him.

"Don't mention it."

Lily was bandaged up and good as new, and we walked back into my house on Lincoln an hour later. Cypress and Rose were sitting at the coffee table with an assortment of colored pencils along with coloring books. Rose had colored a mermaid while Cypress had colored in a garden of flowers outside a cottage.

Cypress got to his feet when he realized I was home. "How are you, princess?" He kneeled down and examined the pink bandage over Lily's arm.

"It's okay," she whispered. "It stings…"

"That'll go away in no time." He pulled her into his arms and gave her a hug. "I used your coloring book. Hope you don't mind."

Lily shook her head. "No."

"But if Mommy used your coloring book, you'd have thrown a fit," I pointed out.

Lily chuckled then walked to the table. She examined Cypress's drawing. "It's pretty."

"Thank you," Cypress said.

Rose pushed her drawing toward her sister. "I did a mermaid."

Lily looked at the picture and pointed to her tail. "Why is it red? It's supposed to be green. Mermaids are green."

"Not all of them," Rose argued.

Cypress watched them for a moment before he turned to me. "Everything alright?"

"Yeah, she'll be fine," I answered. "Thanks for watching Rose."

"She's a piece of cake," he said. "I love spending time with my nieces, so don't worry about it."

"Cake?" Lily looked over her shoulder at the two of us.

"Oh no..." Anytime sweets were mentioned, that's all they wanted.

"Are we getting cake?" Rose asked.

Cypress grinned. "I should watch what I say more often."

"Can we get ice cream?" Rose asked. "We always get ice cream when we're sick."

"But you aren't sick," I said. "Lily is fine."

Lily slammed her fists down. "Ice cream!"

Rose caught on and did the same. "Ice cream!"

Cypress shrugged. "I think we have to give in to their demands or face their wrath."

"Ice cream!" they shouted together, laughing at the same time.

I rolled my eyes and grabbed my purse. "Let's go."

THE GIRLS SAT TOGETHER AND ENJOYED THEIR ICE CREAM, making an enormous mess across the surface. I tried to teach them to be clean, but it never worked. I made my peace cleaning up their mess afterward.

Cypress didn't order anything. He hardly ate sweets.

I didn't have much of a sweet tooth either. "How are you?"

"Good." He always gave me the same answer, but it never seemed like he meant it. I hadn't seen him truly happy in years. I shared the same devastation, but on many different levels.

"How is she?"

He shrugged. "She's had a weird couple of days. When she saw me the other day, she hated me so much...then when she saw me the next day she tolerated me. We had dinner together and kissed at the front door. But then she kicked me out."

I still couldn't believe he put himself through this. "She usually calls me when she realizes you're her neighbor. It never gets easier. Actually, it's been hard lately. I can barely talk to her. It's like she's my sister...but she's just a ghost."

"I know," he whispered.

I tried to stay positive about the situation, but it was getting more difficult. Sometimes I saw my sister at work since we operated and ran several restaurants in the city, but it was never quite the same. I had to lie about my life, about my daughters, about my husband...who was now my ex-husband. "We can't do this forever, Cypress. One day she's gonna be old and know something is off."

"I realize that."

I knew how much Cypress loved my sister. It was the kind of love I'd never witnessed any other time in my life. But it was just unrealistic. "Cypress, I understand how you feel. But no one would judge you if you moved on with your life. You deserve to have a family of your own." I'd mentioned this once before, but he hadn't taken my advice.

He looked out the window of Carmel Bakery, past the shelves of cookies and cupcakes and to the sidewalk outside. Tourists walked past the window, taking a peek at the goodies inside before they continued on their way. "In sickness and in health...that was my promise."

"Cypress..."

"Really, it's okay." He brushed it off like it was nothing, but it wasn't nothing.

I knew Cypress had hope that something would change. Bree had been walking down the street late at night when a driver had a stroke and crashed into her. She didn't have any serious injuries, but she hit her head on the sidewalk. Ever since then, she'd woken up every morning thinking it was three years in the past. The last memory she had of Cypress was the first time they broke up, and frankly, he had been an ass. "The doctors said they have no reason to think her condition will change."

"You don't need to remind me." He crossed his arms over his chest, but he wasn't harsh toward me. He eyed the girls as they continued to make huge messes of their ice cream cones. When he didn't want to talk about it, he changed the subject. "Any improvements with Evan?"

"Nope. Not at all." I was still fighting to get him to pay child support. Since he knew I had money, he said I didn't need him to give me anything. Now he was living with his barely legal wife in Monterey. He'd traded me in for a younger, hotter woman. I would never get over the betrayal. The worst part was, he didn't even take time to see his daughters anymore. It was like he stopped caring about them.

And that was the most difficult part.

Cypress had been more of a father to them than Evan had ever been.

"We're gonna have to take him to court," Cypress said. "It's not about the money. It's about reminding him that he can't just blow off his responsibilities. I'll handle it. I know a few great attorneys."

"Thank you." It was so much easier not doing everything alone.

"No problem."

He pulled up the sleeve of his shirt and eyed the time.

"If you've got it covered here, I think I'm gonna head home."

I knew exactly why. "Of course. Have a good night."

He hugged both the girls before he patted me on the shoulder. "Things will get better. I promise."

4

BREE

Overnight, my yard had gotten out of control. My shrubs needed to be trimmed, my flowers needed sprucing up, and the plants in my window box were getting so tall they blocked most of the sun. I pulled on my gardening gloves and got to work. The sun had been out since seven in the morning, and it made my normally leisurely gardening feel like work. I wiped my forehead with the back of my arm so the sweat wouldn't get in my eyes.

I heard my neighbor's door open and shut next door and then the sound of a jingling collar of a dog. I didn't even know I had a new neighbor. When I looked over my shoulder, I came face-to-face with an Australian Shepherd, his mouth open and his tongue hanging out. He released a quiet whine before he rose on his hind legs and put his paws on my shoulders.

Kind dogs populated the town of Carmel, but I'd never met such a sweet dog. "Hey, boy." I dropped my tools and gave him a good rubdown, scratching his back and behind his ears. He kept his paws on me and drooled onto the soil underneath him. "Aren't you cute?"

He dropped his paws then moved closer into me, shaking his tail enthusiastically and looking at me with his tongue hanging out.

"Wow, you're friendly."

Footsteps sounded next to my yard, and a pair of Keds appeared in my line of sight. "He likes you more than me," a man said with an attractive chuckle. "Traitor."

The guy sounded hot, but that was too good to be true. Most of my neighbors were retired, along with the other residents of Carmel. It was a cute town full of quiet streets and aggressive squirrels. One woman's lawn flamingo was decapitated, and it was all the town could talk about for three months. "He's just a big sweetheart." I looked up, embarrassed that I was in my gardening pants and sporting a bun.

And I looked right into the face of Cypress, the biggest heartbreaker in the world. "Uh...what are you doing here?"

"I live next door." He nodded to the large white house next to mine. "And this is Dino."

"Dino? As in dinosaur?" Wait, I was getting off topic.

"Yeah. He's pretty ferocious."

"A ferocious licker, maybe." I stood up, giving my knees a break from being bent for so long. I gave Cypress another look to make sure it was really him. The last time we saw each other was a year ago. He looked exactly as I remembered. "So...what are you doing here?" I never had fantasies of us getting back together. He was the biggest asshole in the world when he hooked up with Vanessa while I was throwing him a surprise party. He had just given me his key a few days before that, but his gesture of commitment obviously meant nothing.

"Like I said, I live here."

So he was still a smartass. "Why do you live next door to me? And when did you move in?" My initial reaction was fury. I didn't want this guy anywhere near me, not after what he did. But if I got really upset, he would know how much power he had over me. Couldn't let that happen. I had to play it cool as much as possible.

"I moved in recently," he said vaguely. "And this was the only house for sale in my price range that I loved."

"Did you know I lived next door at the time?"

"No. It's a great coincidence. But you know what they say, sometimes things are just meant to be."

I hated it when he flirted with me. The fact that he was so good at it just annoyed me. With perfect good looks like that, he could pull off anything. He wasn't just handsome by normal standards. He was exceptionally beautiful, the kind of man who belonged on TV or in a magazine. That was probably why I used to jump his bones any chance I got. "I doubt our circumstance qualifies..."

He stood in dark jeans and a white t-shirt. He was just as fit as he used to be, judging from his muscular arms, powerful chest, and his long and toned legs. When we were together, he used to run every morning and lift weights every evening. He must still do that regimen. "You wanna get breakfast at La Bicyclette? Dino and I were just about to go."

I couldn't keep my cool any longer. "Sorry, I'm still trying to process the fact that you live next door..."

"Then let's talk about it over breakfast. Come on." He whistled and walked to the road, Dino immediately following without needing a leash. When Cypress reached the road, he turned around. He cocked his head to the side and whistled, signaling to me just the way he did to his dog.

"Are you calling me like a dog?" I asked incredulously.

He patted his thigh. "Dogs are awesome, so don't act like it's an insult."

"I don't have four legs, and I'm not covered in hair—so it is an insult."

"That's debatable." He grinned as though teasing me gave him immense pleasure.

I didn't understand how we could run into each other like this and talk like we were old friends. I should be angry, and he should be embarrassed. But like always, the chemistry was there. Against my better judgment, I joined his side, and we walked up the hill to Dolores.

"I'm starving." He moved effortlessly up the hill, not winded by the steepness. Tourists always had to stop a few times to catch their breath. It seemed like he'd been living there for years rather than days.

"I'm hungry too."

"What are you going to get?"

"Definitely a coffee." I wasn't fully awake yet, and I needed liquid energy to wrap my mind around what had just happened. When I got back to the house, I'd have to call Amelia and tell her the news.

"Not a morning person, huh?"

"I am. I'm just not used to company so early in the day."

We turned on Dolores, and the road finally leveled out, so we walked leisurely and gave our tight calves a chance to relax. When I first moved here, I was achy on a daily basis, but now my body was used to it. "Are you sore?"

"Why would I be sore?"

"You aren't used to walking up and down all the hills. When I first moved here, I was exhausted all the time."

"Oh...not yet."

"It's probably because you're already so fit."

He turned his head in my direction, a smile on his face. "You think I'm fit?"

Instead of feeling embarrassed, I kept my cool. "Well, you obviously aren't out of shape. Anyone with eyes would notice."

"But you're the one with the eyes, and you're the one who noticed." He nudged me in the side with his elbow. "You obviously aren't out of shape either. That's what my eyes are telling me."

Dino walked right beside me, looking up at me every few seconds with his tongue hanging out of his mouth. He always stayed close by and never wandered into the street. "You have a good dog." Steering the subject away from our toned bodies was smart. I hadn't gotten any action in the past year and I was drier than the desert, but I wasn't going to let my hormones get to me. If he had been just a hot next-door neighbor, that would have been fine. But he was my cheating ex—so that was never gonna happen.

"Yep." Cypress looked down at his furry companion. "He's my best friend."

I was such a sucker for men with dogs. Seeing a strong man care for an animal was the biggest turn-on in the world. But I swallowed those feelings down and refused to let them come back up.

We walked inside La Bicyclette, the French restaurant on the corner. It had large oval windows and two old bicycles outside, and it was full of people even on a Tuesday morning. We got a seat on the left side of the restaurant at a small wooden table with even smaller chairs. Cypress looked humongous in it, and I hoped the chairs were sturdy enough to hold his weight. All the waitresses were young, pretty girls in dresses with sneakers. One approached our table and took our coffee order before she walked away.

Dino lay underneath the table, his chin resting on his paws as he surveyed everyone in the room. Chefs in white coats prepared breakfast in plain sight using a wood-burning oven. Eggs sizzled in hot pans, and bread was freshly baked at the same time. This place always smelled incredible. They should charge just to experience the aroma.

Our freshly brewed coffees arrived on silver saucers, along with cream and cubed brown sugar.

Cypress drank his black, exactly as I remembered.

I needed nearly all the cream. I liked my coffee almost white, milky.

Cypress held up the small sheet of paper. "What are you getting?"

I glanced at the menu, and it didn't take long to find what I wanted. "Village combo. I love their poached eggs."

"I was gonna get the French toast, but that sounds pretty good…"

"It's a big decision," I teased. "Take your time."

"I have an idea." He dropped the menu on the table. "We split an order of French toast, and I'll get the Village combo too. You love French toast too. The more syrup, the better."

I was surprised he remembered that. I couldn't even recall when we'd had French toast together. We only dated for three months. "Now that is genius."

Cypress put the order in, and we returned to staring at each other while we sipped our coffees.

I couldn't believe I was sitting across the table from Cypress as if everything was normal. The gang would get a kick out of it when they heard the news. Everyone had hated Cypress after I walked into the restaurant and told them he wasn't coming—because he was busy getting his dick wet. They'd probably judge me for eating with him right then and there.

The fact that we were getting along so well only annoyed me. If he hadn't been a liar and a cheat, I had no doubt we would have ended up together. Despite what he did, he would always have a place in my heart. That was just the vulnerable romantic inside me, but I would never give in to her soft ways. I wasn't stubborn or unforgiving, but I didn't accept anything less than what I deserved. And Cypress didn't deserve me.

"So...what are you doing here?" I held my cup between my fingertips, blew off the steam, and then took a drink.

"I'm pretty hungry," he said with a straight face.

I chuckled just before I took a sip. "In Carmel. When did you leave Monterey?"

The corner of his mouth rose in a smile. "I own a few restaurants here. It's much easier to walk into town and handle business than drive every day."

"You own restaurants?" I blurted. In college, he talked about owning a business someday, but I didn't realize that was his objective, especially in Carmel. It was difficult to start anything in this small town because there were intense restrictions on everything. For instance, corporate chains weren't allowed in the city. Even Starbucks didn't make the cut.

"Yeah, a few. There's a Mediterranean place on Lincoln, and an Italian place on Ocean and Casanova."

I could hardly believe what I was hearing. "I had no idea..."

He stirred his coffee even though he hadn't added anything to it before he took another drink. His shoulders looked broader than I remembered. Maybe he drove to the gym in Monterey every day to lift weights.

The fact that I was doing something really weird with Cypress and it didn't feel weird...was weird. I hadn't seen him in a long time, and we'd ended on such bad terms. I was still hurt by what he had done and would always be scarred by it, but I didn't feel like I wanted to strangle him...at least right now. "Isn't this strange?"

"What?"

"Did you ever think we would be next-door neighbors and having breakfast together?"

"Not quite. But I always hoped our paths would cross again."

Dino moved underneath the table and rested his chin on my foot. I could feel the soft hair brush against my ankle. The dog was particularly comfortable with me even though I was a stranger. "Why would you want our paths to cross?" He'd tried to get me back when we broke up, but after about a week, he gave up.

"I really am sorry about what happened. I wish I could take it back."

But he couldn't. He never could.

"I guess I'd like another chance."

"Another chance?" I asked incredulously. We hadn't spoken in a year, and he wanted to get back together? He didn't even know me anymore.

"Another chance to be your friend," he explained.

"You and I always had a great connection. Seems like a waste to throw it all away."

"Yes, a waste is the best way to describe it," I said coldly.

He brushed off the insult by not reacting to it.

"So...did you move next door to me on purpose?"

"You already asked me that."

"And I'm still suspicious. I'm not the type of person who believes in coincidences."

"Maybe it's not suspicious or a coincidence. Maybe it's fate."

"Fate?" I asked incredulously.

"Yep."

"Fate for me to sell my grandmother's house and move, maybe."

He continued to wear his expression of confidence. It had hardly ever faltered in the time I'd known him. "I'm a very charming guy. I'm easy to talk to, I make you laugh, and I'm a dog lover. I think the two of us could get along pretty well."

"I'm sure we could. I fell in love with you for a reason."

The hard expression in his eyes immediately softened. "Then fall in love with me again."

I forced a laugh even though I was hot and uncomfortable. My body still craved his on a primal level. My attraction for him would never die, despite the scar he left over my heart. He made me weak and strong at the exact same time. If he was going to be my neighbor, I couldn't let myself go weak for him. Friends, maybe. But nothing more. "I think that ship has sailed, Cypress."

"Come on, we all make mistakes. I'm not the same guy I was back then."

"Once a cheater, always a cheater."

He shook his head. "Not true."

"How would you know? Have you really changed that much in a year?"

He clenched his jaw and looked down at his coffee. "Maybe it's only been a year, but it feels like much longer. Yes, I'm a very different man than I was then. I'm the most loyal guy you'll ever meet."

I scoffed even though I felt bad for doing it. "Then the next woman in your life will be very lucky."

"How about if that next woman is you?"

I cocked my head, surprised by his aggression. "You haven't seen me in a year. You don't know me anymore. I could be a weirdo."

"I'm a weirdo too, so that's fine with me."

"You aren't a weirdo," I said with a laugh. There were two women in the corner who had checked him out five different times. They'd sink their claws into him the second they could.

"Then let's make this a date."

"I thought you said we could be friends."

"How about friends who date?"

I rolled my eyes. "Friends only."

"One date. How about that? That sounds fair."

"It would be fair if I owed you something, but I don't." I hadn't even put on my makeup or changed my clothes from gardening, but he was pursuing me like he needed to have me. "There are a lot of beautiful women in this city, especially if you like tourists. You'd have better luck with them."

"I don't want them," he said seriously. "I want you."

I held his gaze until the intensity became too much. I looked away just when the pretty waitress arrived and placed our food in front of us. Poached eggs, tomatoes and greens, and a fresh baguette from the oven, along with thick slices of French toast. It smelled incredible, but the food wasn't enough to make me forget about the awkward situation currently in effect.

Cypress finally broke eye contact when he knew he wouldn't get anything out of me. He set his napkin in his lap then dug into his food, leaning forward and eating like a caveman. He didn't make a mess, he just ate quickly.

"Hungry?" It wasn't the most intelligent thing to say, but it was better than nothing.

"I went on a long run this morning," he said between bites. "Dino did too."

He was still sitting on my foot. "No wonder why he's so tired."

"After a nap, he'll be running around at a million miles an hour again."

We enjoyed our meal, and Cypress didn't mention anything about the two of us getting back together again. He seemed to have exhausted the topic and moved forward. If he thought something would happen on the first day we saw each other, he was arrogant. He could pick up any other woman on their first meeting, but not a woman he cheated on.

When we finished, Cypress slipped cash onto the clipboard and immediately handed it back to the waitress. "Keep the change."

"Wait—" The waitress had already walked away with his money. "I thought we would split it."

"Breakfast is on Dino today."

"Well, if that's the case..." I leaned over and patted Dino on the head. "Thanks for the food."

"He says no problem." Cypress rose to his feet, getting the attention of the two French women at the corner. I assumed they were French because they were whispering to each other in a European language that didn't sound like Spanish.

We left La Bicyclette and walked back home, Dino energized again now that he'd had a short nap underneath the table in the restaurant. We walked side by side, and the sun broke through the cloud bank and poured sunlight onto the city.

We walked toward the water until we reached Casanova then turned left. I made the walk by myself all the time and had never imagined Cypress would join me. Cypress pointed out some wildlife on the way, a loud blue jay and a group of crows sitting on the telephone pole wires.

When we reached our houses, I was relieved the morning was over. While the same chemistry and attraction simmered between us, my walls were so high I had a skyscraper placed in front of me. "Well, I'll see you later. I need to get ready and get to work."

Instead of going up to his front door, he followed me to mine. He got dangerously close to me, his cologne wafting over me. I could see the coarse hair over his chin and the brilliance of his eyes in the sunlight.

I should have just walked inside, but I stood there instead. My neck suddenly felt warm, and my lungs ached for the air I wasn't receiving. My knees felt weak and I wanted to sit down, but I held my ground. I couldn't let my attraction to him cloud my thinking. I hadn't gotten any action for a long time and I wouldn't feel bad for using Cypress, not after what he did to me, but I didn't want it to lead to something else.

Now he was far beyond the friend zone. He backed me up into the door without touching me and pressed his face close to mine. "Thanks for having breakfast with me."

My fingers went numb, and my skin turned searing hot. My back was flat against the door, and my eyes were focused on his full and soft lips. I remembered exactly how our kisses used to be. It was something I couldn't forget even if I tried. I told myself I wouldn't let anything happen, but now my back was literally to the wall and I wasn't doing anything to stop this from happening.

And then it did happen.

His hand snaked into my hair, and he gave me a soft kiss. It was restrained and gentle, feeling natural and sweet. His fingers lightly caressed me then moved down the nape of my neck, brushing against the sensitive parts of my skin. He brought my bottom lip into his mouth and fondled it between his lips, caressing my mouth with purposeful embraces.

So good.

My mouth moved with his, and I wrapped my fingers around his powerful wrists, feeling the corded veins that stretched over the surface. His strong chest was against mine, pressing against my boobs in my top. He inched closer to me until our bodies were completely combined together, hard against my mahogany door.

I knew this wasn't just wrong, but stupid. But in that moment, I didn't care. It'd been so long since I'd had the affection of a strong man. Cypress was the last guy that I slept with, and I'd be lying if I said I didn't miss the incredible sex. He was the best I ever had, hands down.

The longer the kiss continued, the less I cared about the past. I just cared about how well our mouths moved together, how good his strong body felt against mine. All logical thought vanished, and I just enjoyed him.

Cypress moved his hand around my back and opened the front door, knowing it was unlocked without even checking. Our feet tapped against the hardwood floor as he maneuvered me inside, Dino's paws padding against the floor as he joined us.

The sound shattered my arousal, and I had the strength to stop this before it turned into a huge mistake. "Look, this isn't—"

Cypress yanked his shirt over his head and tossed it on the ground. Like a warrior carved from stone, he was all muscle and flawless skin. He had strong, wide pecs that led to an eight-pack that was harder than the wood floor. Endless lines of muscle covered his body, and his well-formed shoulders and upper arms were just as tight.

My mouth dropped open, and I couldn't stop staring.

Damn, he was hot.

Like, H-O-T kinda hot.

Cypress stared at me with the same intensity as before, waiting for the opportunity to crush his mouth against mine again.

Now I didn't care if this was a bad idea. I'd probably think it had been a mistake tomorrow. Oh well. "Never mind."

He charged me again and grabbed a fistful of hair at the back of my head. He kissed me hard, his erection outlined through his jeans and his arousal obvious in the heat of his kiss. Somehow, he knew my bedroom was upstairs because he scooped me into his arms and carried me up the three levels to my bedroom at the top. My arm was hooked around his neck, and I kissed the corner of his mouth as he carried me, listening to his heavy breathing as he worked to get me into the bedroom as quickly as possible.

He set me on the bed then stripped off his jeans, working fast as if he hadn't gotten any action in a long time. He didn't hesitate before he pulled down his boxers and revealed his impressive length. Still long and thick, it had never looked more appetizing to me.

He moved to me next and yanked my shirt over my head before he snapped my bra open within a heartbeat. He kissed me and pushed me onto my back before he yanked off my shoes and tugged at my pants until they were in a ball on the floor. When he took off my panties, he didn't hesitate either. It was like he was afraid I would change my mind if he moved too slowly.

No way in hell was I changing my mind now.

With his perfect naked body, he crawled on top of me and spread my thighs with his knees. His weight dipped the bed, and his thick muscles tightened and looked even sexier. They bulged with masculine strength, and I had to fight the urge to plaster kisses all over his body.

He leaned far over my body and locked eyes with me as he pressed his thick head inside me.

My mind was totally in the gutter, but I still had a grip on reality. "Condom."

Cypress sighed like he was annoyed then got off me and opened my top nightstand drawer. He snatched one and ripped the foil before he rolled it onto his length.

I wanted to know how he knew where they were, but I really didn't care about the answer, so I gripped his arms and pulled him back on top of me.

He returned his hand to my hair where I liked it then slid inside me, pushing through my wetness until every inch was thickly placed inside me. The stretching was incredible. I felt full in every way. Now I knew I would never regret this. How could I regret something that felt this incredible?

He pressed his head to mine and closed his eyes. "Jesus fucking Christ."

I moaned so loud I was embarrassed by my own enthusiasm. I'd given him the cold shoulder at least five times that morning, but now I was fucking him without any reservations.

"Bree..." He gripped my hair tightly and gave me a hard kiss on the mouth.

My arms hooked around his and underneath his shoulders, and I dug my nails into his skin. My ankles locked together, and I took a second to enjoy how incredible it felt. I couldn't remember the last time I'd gotten laid. It was at least a year ago.

Why did I wait this long?

Cypress rocked into me slowly, releasing suppressed moans he couldn't contain. He'd always been good in the sack, but I'd never seen him this enthused, this passionate. "God, you're beautiful." He worked his hips as he locked his eyes on to mine, rocking the bed as he moved back and forth.

"Shit, I'm gonna come..." I dug my nails into him harder, but I didn't have a chance to be embarrassed. The second he was inside me, I was ready to burst. He was either that amazing in bed, or I was going through the driest spell of my life.

Cypress fucked me harder, slamming my headboard into the wall as he drove into me with deep thrusts. The blood pounded into his muscles, making his skin flush and his body slick with sweat.

I'd never seen anything sexier.

I moved my hands up his back until my fingers dug

into his damp hair. His cock felt incredible between my legs, just as it used to when we would screw all over his apartment. No other man had ever made me feel this good in my life. I didn't even think sex was all that great until Cypress came along.

"Come, sweetheart." He gave me a wet kiss, his tongue diving into my mouth and exploring me intimately.

On command, I felt my body tighten around him, and I came with a rush, the heat surging through my body like an erupting volcano. My nails slipped against the sweat coating his skin, and I dug into him harder to keep my grip. I breathed into his mouth as the sensation hit me right in the core, making me melt all over the bed. It was incredible, far better than anything I could do with my own hand. "Cypress…" It felt even more erotic saying his name, making love to a man who seduced me the second he kissed me.

His eyes became lidded and heavy as he watched me. I'd seen that look a hundred times, and I knew what was coming next. His cock thickened inside me just seconds before he burst inside the condom.

When we were together before, we'd never used condoms. I missed feeling him fill me with his seed. It felt so good to watch him give me everything he had. It usually turned me on all over again. Even though a piece of latex separated us now, it didn't stop us from both enjoying it.

He gripped my neck tighter and widened my legs farther with his other arm. He pounded into me harder, grinding against my clit as he slipped through the arousal that seeped from my walls. He gave a low moan as he came, filling the tip of the condom. "Fuck…" He kept his eyes locked to mine, his face even more handsome as he reached his climax.

I didn't have any regrets because I felt so good. Maybe having him next door wouldn't be the worst thing in the world. I could keep him as a fuck buddy when I didn't have any action going on in my life.

He rolled over and pulled off the condom before he tossed it in the trash and put on another one.

I watched him. "What are you going to do?"

He rolled back on top of me and widened my legs farther than last time. "Have you again."

5

Amelia

After I dropped off the kids at school, I went over to Amelia's Place, a diner we owned on Mission Street. Even though it was Thursday, it was packed with locals looking for a good breakfast. I liked the fast-paced environment, but more importantly, the food. I could eat there every day.

When I walked through the door, I saw Cypress at the register. He was doing the books and making a wait list for customers. "Hey. How's it going?"

He had a huge grin on his face. "It's going great. It's a beautiful morning." He shut the register and rolled up the receipts from yesterday.

Cypress was generally pleasant and in a good mood, but he wasn't ever this happy. The last time I saw him in a truly good mood was the day before Bree was in that accident. "Why are you so happy?"

He shrugged. "No reason. Now that you're here, I'm gonna seat the north corner. Is that cool with you?"

I wasn't buying it, but we had customers to serve, and I

needed to get to work. "Yeah, I'm ready." I grabbed my notebook and said good morning to the cooks. Cypress seated the guests, and the busser came over with coffee. Then I walked over and took their order, filling the last waitress shift for the morning.

When I headed back to the kitchen with my orders in hand, I saw Cypress singing under his breath at the register. His wedding band was on his finger, which he usually wore when he was working, and he seemed different. I knew something was up, but I'd have to ask him later.

"What's up?" Blade sat at one of the tables in the corner with his folders covering the surface. He'd already ordered breakfast from the Hippopotamus Café, one of the restaurants we all ran together. Technically, Bree opened it first, but since she didn't have a clue what was going on now, we had to run it for her. Not that we minded. We expanded to other restaurants in the city, and now it was a family business.

Well, most of us weren't related, but we were pretty much family. "Just closed Amelia's Place." I took a seat with Cypress next to me.

Blade had dark brown hair against fair skin. He was tall and toned and wore reading glasses whenever we did paperwork together. He'd been friends with Bree and me for a long time, and Cypress had merged into our group once he'd earned our forgiveness. After they got married, we built our businesses together. "I just went over the orders. Let me know what you think." He handed off the paper to Cypress.

Cypress stared at the sheet, singing under his breath again.

Blade must have known something was off too because he narrowed his eyes. "Why are you in such a good mood?"

"I'm not," Cypress said without taking his eyes off the sheet. But he stopped singing.

Blade exchanged a look with me.

I shrugged in response.

"Bullshit," Blade said. "What's up?"

"Nothing." Cypress turned to the second page. "Everything looks good, but I say we change up the specials. We've been rotating the same ones over and over. Let's do something new."

Blade wouldn't let it go. "You got laid last night, didn't you?"

Cypress's grin grew wider. "Maybe."

"I don't know how you do it." Blade shook his head. "You manage to get your ex to sleep with you in one day after you cheated on her. Unbelievable."

"She's not my ex," he said defensively. "She's my wife."

Bree and I used to be close, but now I felt distant from her. The only time we spoke was when she called to tell me the same thing she told me every day. Now I just went through the motions and tuned her out. It broke my heart that she was gone. She didn't know anything about her nieces. She didn't know Evan was gone. She was just a ghost...and I missed her.

"Whatever," Blade said. "You still have amazing skill. Bree can be so stubborn."

"She has her bad days," Cypress admitted. "But she has her good days too... And it was a really good day." His grin returned.

Blade nodded. "I don't know how you do it, man..."

Blade, Ace, and I had told Cypress to move on multiple times. It couldn't be healthy for him, living for days when Bree would be in an exceptionally good mood so they could spend time together. He repeated the same conversations with her over and over again. His commitment was unbelievable. And as his friend, I worried about it.

"I do just fine," Cypress said quietly. "I know one day, she's gonna come back. And I'll be there when she does."

She wasn't coming back. I knew it.

Blade knew it.

Ace knew it.

But we let him believe this fantasy because it kept him sane. One day, he would finally give up and move on. Of course, we would be there for him when that day came. We would love him like we did now—because he was still family.

Ace was in the back kitchen of Olives, the Mediterranean place we owned on Ocean. When things got busy, he helped out by running food to the table or ringing up customers. The dishes clanked as they were stacked, and the dishwasher worked at full speed to get new plates ready to be served.

"Hey, need help?"

Ace stepped away from the line of hot food and came toward me. In slacks and a collared shirt, he looked as good as gold. He had a handsome face, one with a strong jaw and a sexy smile. Hazel eyes matched the green plants all around Carmel, and he was built like a brick house. "I think I got it. How's the café?"

"Good. We just put in the weekly order and decided on the new special."

"What's it going to be?" He stepped out of the way when a waiter walked by.

"Enchiladas."

"Ooh...sounds pretty good."

"Cypress is experimenting with it as we speak."

"He's a great cook. I'm sure it'll turn out good." He wiped his hands together to knock off the pieces of saffron rice that stuck to his skin.

"Yeah, probably." I didn't really have much to do here since we'd hired a manager to oversee the place. We each had our own territories, and we switched positions depending on our schedules. Since I had kids, I worked while they were at school and sometimes on the weekends when I had a sitter. Managing so many businesses was definitely a team effort, and we divided the profits evenly no matter how much or little we worked.

"Well, I should get back to work." He took another step when one of the workers needed to get past.

"Are you doing anything later?" I tried to find a reason to stick around, but the restaurant was well managed on its own.

"Lady and I are getting some dinner. Why?"

So he was still seeing her. I kinda thought she was a one-night stand type situation. Guess I was wrong. "I was thinking about getting everyone together to make s'mores in my backyard. But maybe another time."

He chuckled. "Like we don't see each other enough as it is."

I forced a chuckle. "Yeah…you're right. Well, I'll talk to you later."

He waved. "See ya."

I walked out of the restaurant and back up Ocean into the Hippopotamus Café. I was stupid for even thinking someone like Ace would want to date a single mom with two kids. He was hot, smart, and hilarious. I'd started seeing Evan when I should have steered clear of him in the first place. But since I got two incredible girls out of it, I couldn't regret it that much.

I walked back into the café where Cypress and Blade were sitting.

"How's Olives?" Cypress asked the second I sat down.

"Good," I said. "Ace didn't need any help."

"That guy is a machine," Blade said. "Most efficient dude I know."

"Yeah…" He was perfect with the customers because he was so charismatic. Everyone thought he was handsome…because he was.

Cypress made a few notes before he left the table. "I'm gonna whip up another batch. Let me know what you think."

Blade gave him a thumbs-up. "Get cooking."

I eyed the empty plate where the first batch of enchiladas had been. "How bad could they have been if you ate them all?"

"They weren't bad," Blade said. "They just weren't different enough."

"People don't want different. They just want good."

He finished what he was writing and looked at me. "Why are you cranky all of a sudden?"

"I'm not," I said defensively.

Blade narrowed his eyes and saw right through me.

"Ace is still seeing Lady... What kind of name is that anyway?"

"I like it."

I rolled my eyes. "You just like it because she has enormous tits."

"Well, I like big tits. Sue me." He turned the page and kept working. When he spoke again, he was much softer. "You want my advice?"

"Always."

"Forget about him. He doesn't see you like that."

He was telling me what I already knew. "I know...I guess I missed my chance. If I'd known he had feelings for me before I started dating Evan—"

"But you did date Evan. And that was a long time ago. He's moved on."

"I know. And he's probably not interested in a single mom with two kids...plus baggage."

"I don't think that's the problem. I just think he's moved on, is all."

Cypress came back, having forgotten his phone on the table. "He's not good enough for you, Amelia. So don't think twice about it." Cypress had turned into a protective older brother even though he was younger than me. It happened even before he married Bree. When Evan left me for that whore, Cypress had marched into his house and broken his nose.

"I thought Ace was your friend?" I asked.

"He is," Cypress said. "He's a great guy. I'd take a bullet for him. But he's not the kind of man you need right now. He's sowing his seeds and fucking around. He's not looking for anything serious, not that it makes him a bad person. Just don't waste your time with him." Cypress walked away again, disappearing into the back where the kitchen was.

"I agree with him," Blade said. "There are a ton of other great guys out there anyway."

They didn't understand. I was a single mom with two kids. I was on the bottom of the dating list. No one wanted to be a stepdad when they didn't even have kids of their own. I'd had my girls pretty early. My oldest was seven, and I wasn't even thirty yet.

Being a single parent wasn't really that difficult for me. I loved my girls, and they gave me so much joy. But I missed having a man in my life. I missed having good sex. I missed everything about having someone. Evan and I were very happy together until a hot little number walked by and his cock got hard. We were blissful up until that moment, so there was nothing I could have done to prevent it. He suddenly wanted something else, and our marriage ended just like that.

I didn't even see it coming.

Blade watched me as my mind wandered off. "You okay?"

"Yeah, I'm fine," I said quickly. "I zoned out there..."

He glanced at the kitchen to make sure Cypress wasn't coming back. "Do you think we should talk to Cypress about everything again?"

I'd already told him several times to move on, but he never listened to me. "Just leave him alone. It's a personal decision. One day he'll realize he needs to walk away. Until then, there's nothing we can do."

"I feel bad for him."

"I do too..."

"He probably only gets laid, like, once a month. Could you imagine living like that?"

I hadn't gotten laid in a year. "Yeah…must not be fun."

"I know marriage is more important than just sex…but he doesn't seem to be getting anything out of it. I hope he doesn't stay because he feels obligated or he thinks we'll lose our respect for him or something."

"No, that's not it," I said quickly. "I told him I would understand if he wanted to leave her and get remarried. He deserves to have his own family."

"Yeah, definitely."

Cypress returned with a plate of enchiladas in red sauce. "Peppers, cheese, and chicken. Give it a try."

We grabbed our forks and each took a bite.

"I like it," I said. "There's something else in it…"

"Spices," Cypress explained. "A lot more cumin, and oddly enough, onion powder."

"I like it," Blade said. "Let's put it on the menu."

"Awesome." Cypress sat down and pulled out his phone.

Blade took another bite then looked around the restaurant, making sure everything was running smoothly. When his eyes focused on something specific, he looked like they might fall out of his head. "Shit. Code red."

"There's a fire?" Cypress asked as he looked at the sprinklers in the ceiling.

"No," Blade whispered. "Bree just walked in."

"Oh shit." I turned around and saw her heading straight for the counter so she could get to work. Sometimes she showed up, prepared to work like it was any other day. Sometimes she assumed it was her day off and didn't come in at all.

"Goddammit." Cypress jumped from the chair and immediately headed out the other entrance so he could escape without being seen.

Bree walked up to our table when she noticed us, but her eyes followed Cypress as he slipped out the door. "Who was that?"

Blade and I exchanged a look before I answered. "Just the health inspector."

"I didn't know he was coming today." She finally turned her gaze back to us and took the seat Cypress had just been occupying.

"I didn't know either." I lied to her so much that now it was effortless. I didn't even feel guilty about it. "But we got a great score, so we're good."

"That's awesome." Bree's brown hair was pulled into a braid. She and Cypress had hooked up yesterday, but she didn't have any memory of it. It made me sad to see how happy Cypress was over a memory Bree couldn't even maintain. "What are you guys working on?"

"The special for the week," Blade said. "We're thinking of doing chicken enchiladas."

"Ooh…" Bree grabbed Cypress's fork and took a bite. "It's pretty good. I'd eat that."

"That's what we just agreed on," I said.

Bree turned to me, and her eyes narrowed on my face. "Everything alright?"

"Yeah," I lied. "Why?" Even now, I felt like I was talking to a ghost. She was there, but not truly.

"You seem slimmer than when I last saw you…but that can't be possible."

Actually, it was. I lost some weight because of the divorce. It wasn't intentional, just a product of depression. I needed to start working out and toning my body. I was thin, but my body was unremarkable.

"I changed my hair." I twirled my fingers through it. "That's probably what you notice."

Bree stared at me longer, her mind searching for a possible explanation for the slight changes around her. One day, she would wake up and twenty years of her life would have gone by. She wouldn't even recognize herself in the mirror. Now she was beginning to pick up on the changes, but they weren't profound enough to send her into a panic.

I hated seeing her like this. It never got easier.

Bree must have finally believed me because she turned around and looked back at Blade. "What can I do to help?"

6

BLADE

I walked into Cultura and saw Ace at the bar. He already had a frosty bottle of beer sitting in front of him, and the baseball game was showing on all the TVs against the wall. I walked across the restaurant and joined him. "Sorry I'm late."

"I hope it's a good story. Like, two women wanted to have a threesome on your way out the door, and you couldn't resist. If that's the case, I totally understand, and I want to hear every single detail."

"If that were the case, I wouldn't have shown up at all." I got the bartender's attention and ordered the same thing Ace was drinking.

"I invited Lady to join us. Is that cool?"

He'd already invited her, so I guess it had to be. "You guys getting serious, then?"

"Why would you say that?" He wore a gray t-shirt with a black jacket. The sun had left the horizon, and now a chilly draft filled the air.

"Don't you introduce a woman to your friends when it starts to get serious?"

"I wouldn't say it's serious. We're just hanging out."

I'd never told him that Amelia was interested in him. I was as much of a friend to her as I was to Ace, and I couldn't spill her secrets unless I had her consent. But Ace didn't seem interested anyway. He would have mentioned something to me if he was. Amelia had dropped a few hints, but he never took the bait. He used to be really into her in high school before she got with Evan. That was a lifetime ago, so it was unrealistic to expect him still to have feelings for her. Plus, she did have two kids. While Ace loved her girls, I doubted he wanted to be a stepfather.

"She's really cool," he said. "She's a bartender in Monterey and goes to school."

"School for what?"

"Psychology, I think."

"Cool…" Sounded a little boring to me, but who was I to judge? I didn't have anyone in my life. I was talking to this woman a few months ago, but it never turned into anything. She was a lot older than me, and I thought I could do the cougar thing, but I wasn't into it.

"That's her." He turned to the entrance as she walked in.

She walked up to him with a smile on her face then wrapped her arms around his neck and kissed him.

When the kiss went on, I turned away so I didn't look like a pervert.

Ace finally pulled his tongue out of her mouth and introduced me. "Lady, this is Blade."

"Nice to meet you," she said as she shook my hand. She was dressed in a short dress and heels, and her hair looked nice. She was definitely a perfect ten. I understood why Ace had kept her around for so long.

"You too." I dropped my hand and nodded to the bar. "What are you drinking?"

"I can buy her a drink," Ace said. "But thanks anyway."

"Ooh…big man," I teased. "He's intimidated because I've stolen a lot of women from him in the past."

"Shut the hell up," Ace said with a laugh. "The only women you've ever stolen are in my *Playboys*."

"You're right," I said as I rubbed my chin. "And they were amazing in the sack."

Lady laughed before she sipped her drink. "Is that all you guys ever do? Make fun of each other?"

Blade and I exchanged a look before we both nodded. "Pretty much."

Cypress walked in the door a moment later in black jeans and a black t-shirt. He obviously hadn't had good luck with Bree if he was turning up here. Sometimes he could turn on the charm and manage to seduce her into the sack. I wasn't sure how, but he obviously had serious game. "What's up?" He fist-bumped both of us. "Lady, right?"

"Yep. Nice to meet you."

He fist-bumped her too. "Cypress." He moved to the counter beside me and ordered a dark beer. "So, what's on the agenda for tonight?"

"Just drinking beer," I said. "Not much else."

"I can get down with that plan." Cypress clinked his beer against mine.

"How was Bree today?"

He shook his head. "It was a bad day. She looked at me like I was the spawn of Satan. I didn't even bother. Maybe tomorrow she'll be better."

"I'm surprised she deviates so much."

"We all have good days and bad days that can't really be explained. If Amelia were the first person she saw in the morning, she'd probably be normal. But since she hates me for what I did…I can't really blame her."

I doubted I would ever love anyone enough to go through that. "I have to hand it to you, man. I couldn't do it."

"Yes, you could," he said simply. "If you found the right woman, you would do anything for her."

I wasn't even in love with Bree, and seeing her like that broke my heart. In my eyes, she was essentially dead. She was doomed to repeat the same conversations every single day. It was a form of torture. "I don't know. I don't think a lot of people would be able to do what you're doing."

"You'd be surprised." He watched the TV as he drank his beer.

Ace and Lady started to make out right against the bar, not caring what anyone thought.

Cypress turned his back to them so he wouldn't have to look at it. He wore his black wedding ring like he did every other day. He never wore it around Bree because that would just make things worse.

"I'm surprised you wear that."

"Why?" He turned his hand over as he examined it. "I am married."

"I know, but it's so complicated."

"I don't want women to think I'm available."

I couldn't do it. If I was gonna be committed to one woman, I wanted sex on a regular basis. "I'm not trying to be mean, and I respect your dedication, but…how can you handle not getting laid all the time?"

"I jerk off a lot," he said honestly.

I shook my head. "Not the same."

Lady pushed up on Ace, scooting closer into Cypress.

Cypress quickly stepped away and wiped off his shoulder like they rubbed something disgusting on him. "Ace, you have a beautiful house down the road. Why don't you take off for the night?"

Ace didn't break his kiss before giving Cypress the finger.

Cypress rolled his eyes.

Ace put cash on the counter. "You're right. We're gonna take off."

"What the hell?" I asked. "I thought we were hanging out?" I didn't want to be a clingy friend, but I didn't appreciate being blown off.

Ace came closer to me and lowered his voice. "It's okay...it's a bro thing."

"A bro thing?" I asked.

He leaned closer. "Lady wants to have a threesome. She has a cute friend, apparently."

That definitely fit into the bro code. I raised my hand to give him a high five. "Good luck."

Ace grinned. "Thanks."

"Want some advice?" Cypress asked.

"I know what I'm doing," Ace countered.

"Fine." Cypress drank his beer and didn't press it.

Ace stood there, his eyes shifting back and forth as he considered it. "Okay...what's your advice?"

We both knew Cypress had been around the block a few times. He had been a serious manwhore and only got his shit together when he found Bree. Even though she was mentally unstable, she still had some invisible power over him.

"Alright." Cypress set down his beer. "Being with two

women isn't much different from being with one woman. But you've gotta be equal. You know what I mean?"

I certainly didn't.

Ace looked just as confused. "Uh...no."

He sighed like we were both idiots. "Most of the time, women are only doing the threesome because it's a turn-on for the guy. They want you, not the other woman. So don't make one wait around too long. Make her come quick, and then bounce back to the other woman. Make her come and bounce back. Most men don't know this, but threesomes are actually a lot of work."

"Hmm…" That was all Ace had to say. "When do I get to come?"

Cypress shrugged. "After they're both satisfied. You're working for them, really." He tapped him on the shoulder. "Go get 'em."

Ace finally walked away and caught up with Lady by the door.

Cypress sighed. "They grow up so fast, don't they?"

I'd never had a threesome. It was something that had just never come up. When other guys said it happened to them, I assumed they were lying. But I knew Cypress was being honest. I'd seen his whorish way with my own eyes. "So, back to what I was saying about Bree. You can really handle that?"

"Don't have any other choice, right? Besides, I have tons of dirty videos we used to make together. It's not like I don't have material."

"But it's still not a marriage."

He drank his beer as he stared at me with irritated eyes. "You've all made your opinions clear about Bree. So now you need to let it go. This is my life. I'll live it how I want."

"I meant well, man. I just want you to be happy."

He nodded. "I know."

"I love Bree. I've known her forever. I wish things could be different, but it doesn't seem like they ever will be."

"But they could," he said quietly. "There's always hope."

Not much.

"Besides, let's say I did move on. I moved to another city and started over. Got remarried or something. What if she got better and then came to me? What would I do? I'd be stuck with someone else, and I couldn't just walk away. And that regret would eat me up for the rest of my life. It doesn't matter how amazing the next woman is. She'll never be Bree. I don't want anyone but Bree. When I argue with her outside the house, it still feels real. It reminds me of all the fun we used to have. She still smiles and laughs the same way. Yeah, maybe it's annoying to have the same conversation over and over again...but it's still her."

Now I felt bad for bringing it up. "I'm sorry. I never should have said anything."

"It's okay," he whispered. "I know you guys are just looking out for me. But I'd honestly rather have some of her like this than nothing at all. Yes, there are nights when I'm lonely as fuck and I wish she was there beside me. Yes, there are times when I want to strangle her because she hates me so much. But it's still better than being with someone else."

I patted his shoulder. "Maybe she'll get better. Maybe she'll wake up one morning, and it'll come back to her."

"God, I hope," he whispered. "I pray for that every fucking night."

7

BREE

I ran out of coffee for my French press, so I decided to get a cup of joe from the coffee shop off Ocean. I walked outside my house into the sunshine and saw my new neighbor walk out of his house. He must have just moved in because I didn't even know the house had sold.

He had an Australian Shepherd with him, black and gray mixed with patches of white. When he reached the end of his driveway, he looked over at me like he'd been expecting me.

And I certainly wasn't expecting him—Cypress.

What on earth was he doing next door? "Uh...what the hell?"

"Good morning to you too." He waved and wore a friendly smile even though nothing about this was friendly. He walked to the bottom step of my stone stairs and crossed his arms over his chest. "What a surprise. I didn't realize you were my neighbor."

"You don't look surprised," I countered. I stayed at the top of the steps, fighting the bile that rose up my throat.

This man broke my heart in the most brutal way possible. "Is Vanessa my neighbor too?" It was a cold jab, but I didn't care. He threw away something incredible to fuck a woman he'd already fucked a hundred times. He broke up with her for a reason, but he screwed her while I threw him a surprise birthday party. Totally sickening.

He took the insult with confidence. "Nope. Haven't talked to her in a long time."

"I'm glad she was worth throwing me away for, then."

He sighed but didn't make a comeback. "It's beautiful here. I really like the house, and I love yours too."

I didn't want to make small talk. "Why did you move here?"

He cocked his head to the side. "I have a business here. Easier to live in town."

So he wasn't going away anytime soon. "Did you really have to move right next door to me? Did I do something to you?"

"It was purely coincidental."

"Bullshit."

"How would I know otherwise?" he challenged. "The realtor said all the neighbors are really nice. And that was it."

I couldn't believe this was happening. The man I despised was next door. "Great, I have to sell my house."

"Come on," he said with a laugh. "I'm not that bad. I can always help around the house if you ever need it. I'm very quiet. I'll keep an eye on your stuff if you're ever gone."

"And I have to watch you bring home tramps every Friday and Saturday night. That should be fun."

He tightened his jaw.

"I don't want anything to do with you. It's pretty rude

to disturb my life like this. I didn't do anything to you. You are the one who broke my heart, not the other way around. Just leave me in peace, alright? You've done enough damage."

He put his hands in his pockets and stared at the ground.

"Hello?"

"Hmm?" he said without looking at me.

"Aren't you gonna say something?"

"No, I'm not. It's just not a good day." He walked back to the house and patted his thigh. "Come on, boy."

"You're right. It's a very bad day."

He didn't look at me again as he walked up to his front door, ignoring me.

He caught me off guard, and now he was the one to walk away? What an asshole. I walked up the stairs, angry and slightly shaken, and my foot slipped on the stone. It must have rained the night before because it was still slippery. I tripped then fell, screaming on the way down. I hit my head against the stone.

Then everything turned black.

"BREE!" CYPRESS'S DISTRESSED VOICE CAME INTO MY EAR.

My eyes fluttered open, and I saw his white house come into view. The sunlight was still bright like I remembered. I could hear a blue jay cry out in the distance.

"Bree?" Cypress gripped my shoulder and helped me sit up. "Can you hear me?"

"Yeah..." I rubbed my skull and closed my eyes, feeling a slight headache coming on.

"I'm gonna call an ambulance. Just sit there, alright?" He pulled out his phone.

"I don't need an ambulance." I pushed his phone down. "I'm fine. I just knocked my head. I'm not even bleeding."

"You still had a pretty bad fall. I should call."

"I certainly don't need an ambulance. Really, I'm fine."

He still looked terrified, like I'd fall apart at any moment.

"Cypress, really." I slowly rose to my feet and felt the ache in my skull. It hurt, but I didn't think there was any permanent damage.

"Let me take you to the hospital." He grabbed both of my hands like I might trip and fall all over again.

I yanked my hands away, repulsed by what he had done to me. I would never get the image of Vanessa riding him out of my head. "I'm fine. I'm just gonna have some water and lie down for a bit."

He got the door open for me and walked inside my house without being invited.

"What are you doing?"

He grabbed a bottle of water from the fridge then propped up the pillows on the couch. "Lie here. I'll get a blanket."

"I don't need you to help," I argued. "Just go, Cypress."

"Stop being so fucking stubborn," he snapped. "You fell down and hit your head on solid stone, alright?"

"Which was your fault."

"My fault?" he hissed. "I was walking back into my house, and you were being careless."

"I was being careless because my new neighbor is a fucking asshole." I lay back on the couch and crossed my arms over my chest.

He shook his head and set the bottle of water on the table. "You really woke up on the wrong side of the bed this morning, huh?"

"What the hell is that supposed to mean?"

"Nothing." He sat on the edge of the coffee table and watched me.

"Why are you still here?"

"Because I need to watch you. Make sure you're okay. You know, because I'm a good human being."

"A good human being? Do good human beings—"

"Stop while you're ahead. I feel terrible for what I did, and I wish I could take it back. I've said that a million times."

"Have not."

"Well...it feels like I have."

I kept my arms crossed over my chest and looked out the window.

He grabbed the blanket from the end of the couch and draped it over me.

"It's seventy degrees outside. I'm not cold." I kicked the blanket back.

He sighed in irritation. "You want some painkillers?"

"I really don't feel that bad."

"Well, I think you're full of it. I'd be in agonizing pain if I slammed my head against stone like that."

"Maybe you're a pussy, then."

He squeezed his hands until his knuckles turned white. "How about I call Amelia and have her come down and watch you?"

"I don't need to be watched by anyone. I'm fine."

He dragged his hands down his face. "That's it. I'm taking you to the hospital. We're gonna at least get your head scanned to make sure you're alright."

"Totally unnecessary—"

"Get your ass up. Now."

"What makes you think you can tell me what to do?"

"Oh, believe me, I have every goddamn right to tell you what to do. Get up and let's go. It's either that or I'm calling the ambulance. It's your call."

I knew he would call an ambulance. He wasn't bluffing. "Fine."

Cypress had me sit down while he checked in at the front desk. A few minutes later, they took me to get a scan done then put me in a waiting room. Cypress sat in the corner while I sat on the bed. We didn't speak.

Thankfully.

I never thought this was how my day was gonna go. I woke up that morning like it was any other day, and then it turned into complete and utter shit. I didn't care about hitting my head against the stairs. I just cared that I was cooped up with this guy.

Cypress sighed then tapped his fingers against his bicep. He didn't look at me.

"You don't have to stay here. I can take an Uber home."

His sigh implied he didn't want to be there. "Don't worry about it."

"Just go, Cypress. I don't like you anyway."

"I'm aware."

The doctor knocked before he came inside. "Mrs. Heston, I've got your test results back…"

Mrs. Heston? That was Cypress's last name. "No, we aren't married. He's just a…friend." I couldn't exactly say my ex and enemy. Sounded kinda weird.

The doctor flipped through my chart. "Uh…"

Cypress tapped him on the arm and then shook his head.

The doctor seemed to understand something because he looked back through the chart and then cleared his throat. "My mistake. Anyway, your test results came back normal. So everything is in the clear. You don't have a serious injury, just a minor concussion."

"What a surprise…" I shot Cypress a glare.

"Better to be safe than sorry," Cypress said back.

"So, you're free to go." The doctor shook my hand then walked out.

"Great," I said. "That cost me a bunch of money for no reason."

"It's called health insurance," he said coldly. "That's what it's for."

We left the hospital, and he drove us home in his two-seater Jaguar. He pulled into his driveway then walked me to my front door.

"You don't need to walk me. I'm fine. Really."

He finally stopped following me. "You're welcome, by the way."

I suddenly felt bad, understanding I was acting like a jerk. Even though I was pissed he was my new neighbor, he'd been considerate and took care of me even when he didn't have to. He could have just called an ambulance and walked back into his house. "Thank you."

He stopped walking and looked at me, somehow recognizing my sincerity. He could have been a jerk back to me, but he wasn't. He gave a slight nod then continued walking to his house. "If you need anything, please let me know." He walked into his house and shut the door.

I apologized, but it still didn't feel good enough. I

walked inside my house and looked at the painkillers my doctor had prescribed me. I truly felt fine, not in any discomfort at all. The scan to my head was totally unnecessary.

I had been planning to go on a walk along the beach, but now, I decided to stay inside. Even though I was fine, it was probably smart to take it easy.

Like Cypress said, it was better to be safe than sorry.

8

BREE

I woke up the next morning feeling just as good as the day before. I rubbed my head and felt a slight bump under my fingertips, but it was nothing to be alarmed about. I brushed my teeth and took a shower instead of going downstairs right away.

Now that Cypress was my neighbor, I couldn't look like hell all the time. He could see me through my big windows, and I couldn't go down the street to get coffee if there was a possibility he might see me.

I shouldn't care what he thought of me. It's not like I would ever get back together with him. But I still needed to keep my dignity as much as possible and prove that I was doing just fine without him. He seriously broke my heart when the shit hit the fan, and I did the best I could to appear calm about the whole thing.

I couldn't let all that hard work go to waste.

I showered and did my hair before I pulled on dark jeans and a gray long-sleeved shirt that framed my curves.

My hair was styled in open curls, and I did my makeup a little heavier than usual.

For not caring, I was putting in a lot of effort.

I walked downstairs and looked at his house through my open windows. He had a white house with white shutters that opened up over his yard. My house had a distinctly different style, Spanish with brown windows and beige stucco. I had a fire pit in the backyard along with stone bricks comprising the patio. An assortment of exotic flowers were sprinkled in the backyard, giving me privacy from my other neighbors.

I didn't see any action going on from his windows, so I grabbed my purse and walked outside. I was out of coffee, and I needed to get a hot cup of joe from the café down the road before I could really get my day started. I didn't go to work yesterday, so I definitely needed to stop by today and check up on some things.

I walked outside and down the driveway just as he appeared, coming up the street with his dog beside him. He was in a t-shirt and running shorts, and the fabric around his neck was dark from the sweat that had formed. He met my look and stopped when he reached the front of his house. "Morning."

"Morning." I crossed my arms over my chest, suddenly feeling tense now that I was around him. Even covered in sweat with a tight t-shirt, he looked unnaturally handsome. When he wore shorts, his thick and muscular legs were clearly visible. I always thought he had nice legs, along with everything else.

He walked forward, and his dog ran up to me, his tongue hanging out.

I expected him to ask me how I was doing, and I was

surprised when he didn't. Maybe he was mad about yesterday.

"Didn't realize you were my neighbor."

I raised an eyebrow, having no idea what that meant. "What do you mean?"

He cocked his head to the side, his eyebrow raised. "As in, I live next door." He nodded to the house. "I just bought it."

Didn't we establish this yesterday? And that was why I hit my head on the stairs. "I know…you said that yesterday."

His eyes snapped open like I'd just said something terrifying. He even took a step back, his hands moving to his hips. "You…you remember yesterday?"

"How hard do you think I hit my head?" I asked incredulously. "Of course, I remember yesterday. We spent two hours at the hospital and got a scan that didn't even show anything." I had intended to come out here and speak to him calmly, but with him acting like I was an idiot, that was pretty difficult to do.

He suddenly marched toward me, his hand extended and his finger pointed right at my chest. "Wait…so you remember hitting your head on the stairs yesterday?"

"Did I not make that clear?"

He stepped back and gripped his scalp. "Oh shit."

"What?" Now he was just acting like a weirdo. "Oh shit, what?"

He paced in a circle and dragged his hands down his face. "Because you hit your head again…so fucking simple. Why didn't I think of that?"

Now I was freaked out. "What the hell are you mumbling, Cypress?"

He finally stopped circling. "I can't believe this…I can't."

"Can't believe what?"

He put his hands on his hips and steadied his breathing. He struggled to keep himself calm, but I didn't know what there was to be worked up about.

"I don't know what the big deal is, but I'm fine. My head and I are fine."

"Do you remember the day before yesterday?"

"Of course I do."

"Then what happened?"

"Why?"

"Just tell me," he hissed. "Please."

When he looked at me with those fierce eyes, I couldn't deny him. "Uh…I went to work with Amelia. It was payday…" Nothing more specific came to mind.

That didn't seem to be the answer he wanted. "Did you see me that day?"

"No. I didn't know you moved in until yesterday."

He nodded his head slowly. "Gotcha…so you don't remember anything."

"Don't remember anything? Yes, I remember a lot."

"Never mind," he said quickly. "We need to talk."

"What are we doing now?"

"Or wait… Maybe I should wait. Just to make sure."

"Wait to make sure of what?"

"Nothing." Cypress stepped back. "Just forget I said anything."

"Maybe I should since none of it made sense."

"I've gotta go. I'll talk to you tomorrow." He walked back toward his house, his dog following behind him.

What the hell just happened?

9

Amelia

I was doing the dishes at the counter while the girls colored in their books at the kitchen table.

A knock sounded on the door then Cypress walked inside without being invited. He was welcome in our home, but I'd never seen him burst inside without warning like that. Blade came in behind him.

"Dude, what is this about?"

"Yeah?" Ace asked. "In case you didn't notice, we have businesses to run."

"They'll survive," Cypress said. "This is way more important."

I wasn't wearing any makeup, and I was just in my sweats and t-shirt. If I'd known they were coming over, I would have done myself up a lot better. I guess I didn't care about Cypress and Blade…just Ace. "What's going on? Everything alright?" I turned off the water and wiped my hands on the kitchen towel.

Cypress paced back forth and gripped his skull at the same time. "This is big, guys. Fucking huge."

"Shh," Ace snapped. "The kids, Cypress."

"Whatever." Cypress stopped walking and looked at us. "Yesterday, Bree and I had an argument—"

"And you got laid?" Blade asked. "Yeah, we've heard it before."

"Shut up before I punch you." Cypress stared him down with his cold gaze, his words not a bluff.

Blade sighed. "Then get on with it."

"She hit her head on the stairs," Cypress said. "I took her to the hospital, and they did a scan. Everything was normal. But when she woke up this morning…she remembered everything that happened yesterday."

I actually got chills. My arms prickled as my hair stood on end. A cold draft entered the house, and all I could hear was the background noise of colored pencils against paper.

Blade was in shock too. He stared at Cypress like he hadn't heard anything.

Ace covered his mouth with his hand, his green eyes expressing the disbelief we all felt.

I was the first one to come up with a response. "She remembered?"

"Yeah," Cypress said with a nod. "She remembered me. She remembered the fall. She remembered all the details."

"Did you tell her who you were?" Blade blurted.

"No," Cypress said. "I was going to take her inside my house and show her everything but…what if it's not permanent? What if she forgets everything tomorrow? I wanted to give it another day to make sure it's not a fluke."

"I doubt it's a fluke," I said. "It's just like the first time she hit her head. It's permanent."

"Fuck, I hope so," Cypress said under his breath.

Ace shot him another glare. "What did I just say?"

"Ace, it's okay," I said. "We're under extreme circumstances." My girls had heard every cuss word under the sun, and they knew it was wrong to repeat them.

"I'm their uncle. You aren't," Cypress snapped. "I can say whatever I want."

"I'm their uncle too," Ace said defensively. "Asshole."

"Me too," Blade said. "Don't pull that marriage card out."

As cute as it was that they were fighting over my daughters, it was unnecessary. "Guys, forget the girls. Let's focus on Bree right now."

"What do we do?" Ace said. "Wait until we see what happens tomorrow?"

"She's going to call me," I said. "I'm surprised she hasn't done it already."

"If she does, just act like everything is normal," Cypress said. "If she remembers everything tomorrow…I'll figure out what I'm going to do."

Ace opened the fridge and grabbed a beer. He twisted off the cap before he took a drink. "Are you just gonna tell her everything?" He leaned against the counter and crossed his ankles. "That's a pretty heavy first conversation."

"It is," Blade said in agreement. "You tell her you've been married for the last two years, and she'll flip. The last thing she remembers is you sleeping with some other chick. She probably won't even believe you."

"We're all the proof she needs," Amelia said. "It'll be hard, but she'll come around."

Cypress crossed his arms over his chest and looked out the window. His chest rose and fell heavily, and his eyes were filled with a million emotions. "I'm gonna get my wife back..." He covered his face with his hands and took a deep breath. When he pulled his hands down again, his eyes were wet and reflective.

Blade walked over to him and patted him on the back, silently comforting his friend.

"Almost there, man." Ace set down his beer and stood on his other side. "You didn't give up on her. Now everything is gonna be alright. No more getting laid once a month."

Cypress chuckled, dispelling the emotion in his eyes. "Yeah, that'll be nice."

"And I'll have my sister back," I whispered. "My nieces will have their aunt back. It's gonna be such a shock to her...all the time she lost. We'll all have to be patient."

"We will," Ace said. "She was always an amazing friend to us. We'll give her all the time she needs."

Cypress looked at me, and I knew what was coming next. He crossed the kitchen and wrapped his arms around me, giving me a bear hug that was both emotional and joyful. He rested his chin on my head and released a quiet sigh. "We're finally getting her back."

I squeezed him hard. "I know."

10

Bree

Now all I could ever think about was my obnoxious neighbor. I wondered when he was home and what the probability of me running into him was. I had always thought Cypress was a great guy. I did fall in love with him for a reason. But when I caught him getting birthday sex from some other woman, when he'd just had sex with me earlier that morning, I was so out of my mind livid.

I really wanted to kill him.

All the respect I had for him vanished in that minute. I felt used and worthless. I was doing something sweet for him, and he was screwing his ex. I didn't put up with cheaters—ever. But that didn't mean I couldn't be civil to the guy.

It wasn't like he was evil.

He was still a good person.

But once a manwhore, always a manwhore.

Simple as that.

I got ready for the day then walked outside. I never locked the front door because there was no necessity. The only kind of crime that happened around here was petty, like people leaving trash on the beach. I had reached the bottom step when Cypress emerged out of his house.

"Hey." He walked down his steps and reached the road, and his dog was nowhere in sight. "Good morning."

"Good morning."

"How's your head doing?" Today, he was in black jeans and a dark blue t-shirt. The dark colors looked great against his fair skin.

"Good. Haven't needed any painkillers, so I can't complain."

He stood in front of me and placed his hands in his pockets. He gave me a look that was different from all the previous ones he'd given me. He stared at me without blinking, like he was staring right into my soul.

I had no idea what had brought that on. "Well, I'm gonna head to work. I'll talk to you later."

"Wait, hold on." He came closer to me and pulled his hands out of his pockets. "How about we get breakfast?"

"Why would we do that?" I didn't mean to sound rude, but the question was sincere. "Just because we're neighbors doesn't mean we need to be friends." The last time I saw him, I slapped him across the face and then slammed the door on him. It wasn't exactly good closure.

He clenched his jaw. "No, we don't need to be friends. But wouldn't it be easier if we were friends? We don't have to avoid each other. Plus, we have a lot in common."

"Like what?"

"Well, I'm sexy and you're sexy." He winked.

I rolled my eyes. "I hope we have more in common than that."

"We have great taste in real estate."

I nodded. "True."

"We're both business owners."

"Really? What do you own?"

"That Mediterranean place, Olives. It's on Ocean."

"Oh, cool. I love that place."

"And you own Hippopotamus Café?"

"How did you know that?"

"Amelia told me."

"Oh..." I guess he'd already run into my sister. My sister hated him more than I did. I doubted that conversation went well.

"So, how about breakfast?"

"I was actually going into work right now."

"Well, I'll go with you."

His insistence was alarming to me. He wasn't even this enthused when we were together. "Really, it's okay."

He started walking toward town. "Really, I insist."

I raised both eyebrows before I caught up to him. The only reason I wasn't screaming at him was because he'd been sweet to me when he took me to the hospital. I already told him off when he cheated on me, so I didn't need to keep being rude to him. "What's this about?"

"What's what about?"

"You always trying to spend time with me. I know you aren't an idiot who thinks we could ever get back together, so what's your other reason?"

"Never get back together, huh?" he asked as he turned and walked up the hill.

"Obviously. Not that I'm implying that you want me."

He didn't say anything.

"So what's your reason?"

"Maybe I'm just a nice guy who enjoys your company."

"Nah, that can't be it. I'm a little annoying."

"A little?" he asked with a laugh. "You're a huge pain in

the ass. But you know what? You're also cute as hell. Balances it out."

"Since those are both true, I'll let that go."

He chuckled, and when he did, he wore the cutest smile on his face.

I tried not to be affected by that swoon-worthy grin. I despised him for hurting me, but my body couldn't deny he was the sexiest thing on the planet. I still hadn't met a guy who could compare to him.

When we reached Dolores, we turned left and headed deeper into town. We turned right on Ocean then walked inside Hippopotamus Café, which was already busy with a line of customers. The only time I walked into this place without it being busy was around two in the afternoon. Other than that, there were always people everywhere. Tables needed to be bussed, trays needed to be taken away, and food needed to be prepped.

"How about we eat together before you start?" Cypress asked. "Your poached eggs are amazing."

"Thanks. And you just made my stomach growl."

We ordered our food then sat down with the Polaroid number that hung on the metal stand. We had our cups of coffee, and shortly afterward, they brought our food. Cypress took his coffee black like I remembered. I needed a ton of cream in mine. Otherwise, it was too strong. He had a few bites, but he looked at me the entire time.

"What?" I finally asked.

"You're directly in my line of sight. What else am I supposed to look at?"

"The rest of the restaurant..."

"There's nothing in here as pretty as you are."

I was pathetic for actually enjoying that compliment.

This guy did the unforgivable, and I shouldn't care about anything he had to say. "Seeing anyone?"

"No. You?"

"Not right now. I'm surprised Vanessa isn't still around. Unless she's a booty call type thing."

He sighed quietly to himself.

"I'm sorry, did that annoy you?" I asked incredulously.

"No, I deserved it," he said calmly. "I just wish I could go back in time and take it back. You have no idea how much that memory haunts me."

"I wish that more than you do."

He took another bite before he looked at me. "Yeah?"

"I told you I loved you, didn't I?" I dropped my gaze because I couldn't look him in the eye. "You were the love of my life."

"And you're still mine."

I focused on my fingers, watching the way I moved my fork around the plate. The conversation had become unexpectedly heavy. I didn't know how to get out of it now. "Well, that was a long time ago. All we can do is move on."

"I wish you would forgive me for it."

I drank my coffee because I couldn't get myself to do it. I didn't hate him, but I would never forget how much he hurt me. "Forgiveness is unnecessary. I managed to get over you, and now I'm in a good place in my life."

"You're over me?" he asked quietly.

"What? You thought I would still be in love with you a year later?"

He drank his coffee without breaking eye contact. "I think when you love someone, you never really stop loving them."

"Maybe. But you never loved me if you cheated on me. So what we had was never real."

He bowed his head in shame. "I did love you, sweetheart. It was a stupid mistake. Wasn't worth it at all."

"But yet you fucked her anyway."

He crossed his arms and looked at me apologetically. "I'm not the same guy I used to be."

"I doubt much has changed in a year. Once a cheater, always a cheater."

"Now, that's just not true."

"I have no reason to believe otherwise." If he thought we could have a calm breakfast together, he was ignorant. Cheating exes couldn't be friends, even if they were next-door neighbors.

He pinched the bridge of his nose before he rubbed his palm across his smooth cheek.

I didn't want to sit there with him anymore. I appreciated him for helping me the other day, but we would never move forward. After he'd hurt me, I was a wreck for three months. I'd thought he was the man I would spend the rest of my life with. Instead, he was the man who'd shattered my heart. I'd never been the same since that horrible afternoon. "I should get to work..."

Cypress didn't try to stop me. "Have a good day."

I walked off and ignored him, wanting to get away from him as quickly as possible.

AMELIA CAME INTO THE OFFICE A FEW HOURS LATER. HER hair was pulled up in a loose bun, and she was in jeans and a white top. "Hey."

"Hey." When I looked at her, I thought she seemed different, but I couldn't put my finger on why. She definitely looked thinner, but I wasn't sure how that was possible. Maybe it was just her clothes. "How's it going?"

"Good. The rush finally died down. Do you need any help in here?"

"No. Just doing the orders."

"Actually, I did them the other day." She opened the folder to show the list of items.

"But we do that on Tuesdays. Today is Tuesday."

"Actually...today is Friday." She pointed to the calendar above the desk.

"Oh..." How did I miss that? "Then never mind. That saves me the hassle." I shut the binder.

"True. Now you get off early today." She took the seat against the wall and pulled out a granola bar. Her wedding ring was missing from her left hand, but I assumed she forgot it. Evan hated it when she forgot to wear her ring. She took a few bites and enjoyed her mediocre lunch.

"Why don't you order something here?"

"I get tired of eating the same thing every day. Besides, these are pretty good."

I checked the schedule for next week. "So, you know how I told you yesterday Cypress is my neighbor?"

"Yeah..."

"We got breakfast together today, and he kept bringing up our relationship. I find it hard to believe he wants to get back together, but...I'm not sure why he keeps bringing it up."

She took another bite and kept eating. "Hmm..."

"Don't you think it's weird that he moved next door to me?"

"It's a strange coincidence."

"I don't know if I believe it's a coincidence. I mean, what are the odds of that?"

"Pretty slim," she said with her mouth full. "But I wouldn't worry about it too much."

"Not worry?" This wasn't my sister at all. "You hate him more than I do."

"Hate is a pretty strong word…"

Now this wasn't adding up. "You told me you wanted to rip off his balls and shove them down his throat. Direct quote."

"Well, that was right after it happened. There's been a good amount of time."

"Whatever. If Evan ever did that to you, I'd rip off his balls and set them on fire."

She faltered in mid-bite before she kept chewing.

"How are things with Evan, anyway? Any date nights?"

"Things are good…"

I'd known my sister for a long time. I always knew when something was bothering her. "Amy, what's up?"

"Nothing," she said quickly. "I should get going. I have to pick up the girls."

"From where?" It's not like they were old enough to be in school.

"The sitter." She walked to the door. "Just go easy on Cypress. Losing you was punishment enough."

I couldn't disagree more. "I'll think about it."

By the time I walked home, it was almost sunset. The lights wrapped around the trees on Ocean were on and bright, illuminating the street where everyone walked to their favorite restaurants for dinner.

I wore my dark green jacket as I walked down the hill to my street. My hands were inside my pockets, and I used the remaining light from the setting sun to guide me. In Carmel, there were very few streetlights, so walking in the dark could be difficult. But you could always see the stars at night, so it was a perk.

I turned onto Casanova and walked past the houses until I passed Cypress's. He was sitting on the porch with his dog, sipping a glass of wine. His dog immediate hopped up and ran to me, his tongue hanging out. He jumped up on his hind legs and placed his paws on my stomach and let out a quiet bark.

"Wow, you're very friendly." I kneeled down and gave him a good rubdown. Even though I hated Cypress, that didn't mean I had to hate his dog. He was way too cute. I scratched him behind the ears and got a wet kiss in return. "What's his name?"

Cypress sat with his leg crossed, his ankle resting on the opposite knee. "Dino."

"Ferocious. Doesn't suit him at all, but it's cute."

"I want the other dogs to be afraid of him."

"Good luck with that," I said with a chuckle. I gave the dog another pat before I stood up. I'd seen Cypress earlier in the day, and we didn't end the conversation on the best terms. But if we stuck to being friendly neighbors, we should be able to tolerate one another. Anything more intimate than that was just too complicated. "Have a good night."

He held up an empty glass. "Join me."

"Aren't you sick of me?"

"Never. Now join me."

"How about we just be friendly neighbors who don't spend time together?"

"How about we try to be friends?" He poured the glass and held it up. "The sun is setting. Let's watch it."

Against my better judgment, I walked up the stone steps and sat in the chair beside him. Dino ran up and lay on the stone at our feet, placing his chin on his paws. I grabbed the glass of wine and took a drink. "Pretty good."

"It's new. I just added it to the wine list at the restaurant."

"It's dry, not too dry. Flavorful."

"It goes well with a sirloin."

I watched the sun creep behind the houses and listened to the waves in the far distance. When the sun went down, the city became much quieter. All the visitors packed up for the day and returned to their homes in Seaside and Monterey. "You like living here so far?"

"Absolutely." He swirled his wine before he took a drink. "Nowhere else in the world I'd rather be."

"I love it too. My grandma loved it even more."

He nodded as he stared at the scenery. "How was work?"

"Good. Amelia helped out today."

"Cool." I was a sucker for wine, so I had to pace myself so I wouldn't down the whole glass and pour another.

"I want you to know that I really am sorry about what happened."

Why did he keep bringing it up? "Let's just move on and forget about it."

"I don't want to move on and forget about it. I want you to forgive me."

"Why is it so important to you?" I stared at Dino, who had already closed his eyes and drifted off to sleep.

"Because I'm a sincere person who feels remorse for what he's done. I'm apologizing to you because I mean it."

It would be cold for me to deny him what he asked for. Forgiveness was important. I wasn't perfect either. I hadn't done something as terrible as that, but I didn't have a completely clean record. "I forgive you."

"Do you mean it?" He turned his head my way.

"Yes." If he was going to all this trouble, I was sure he meant it.

"Thank you." He grabbed the bottle of wine and topped me off again. "It means a lot to me."

"Sure…" I felt a little better now that I let it go. It was a long time ago, so there was no reason to keep it in the present. Forgive and forget. "I guess we can try being friends. Maybe friendly acquaintances."

"Yeah…maybe."

We sat in silence as we watched the sun disappear over the horizon. The light faded away until darkness crept in. I had downed two glasses of wine, and I was ready for bed. I had to get up early in the morning for work. "Thanks for the wine…" I set the empty glass on the ground. "I'll see you around." When I stood up, he did the same.

"I'll walk you to your door."

I chuckled because I thought it was a joke. But when I realized he meant it, my laugh faded away. "You can see me from here. I'll be fine."

He stood in front of me and didn't push it. He glanced at the ground between us before he looked me in the eye. The intensity was similar to the way he'd looked at me this morning, when we were outside the house and then again when we were across the table from each other at the restaurant.

It made my skin prickle.

He suddenly moved forward and dug one hand into my hair. His lips maneuvered to mine, and he kissed me.

I should have known this was a trap. I stepped back and pushed his arm down. "Cypress, no."

"Sweetheart…" He used to call me that all the time, especially when we were in bed together.

"I've forgiven you, and I'll be your friend. But that's it. I never want to be with you again."

His eyes narrowed in pain.

"And I definitely don't want to be a fuck buddy, if that's what you were going for."

"I wasn't."

"Well…I've moved on, Cypress. I don't see you that way anymore, and even if I did, I wouldn't be with you. I deserve someone I can trust. And you're the last person in the world that I trust." I hated being so harsh, but I didn't want him to think there was any chance we would ever be together again. We could be friendly since we lived so close to one another, but even that was a stretch for me.

"I can earn your trust back if you give me a chance."

"I don't have to give you a chance, and I don't want to. Don't kiss me ever again. Next time, I'll slap you." I wasn't bluffing. If I had it my way, he wouldn't even be living next door to me. I'd finally stopped thinking about him six months after we broke up. My heart had healed, for the most part. I didn't want to rip it open again, especially when there wasn't much left. Maybe I could forgive him, but I could never forget what he did to me.

"I know you still love me." He spoke with complete confidence. As if there was no possibility he could be wrong. It was a bold statement.

"I don't, and I don't have any idea why you think I might."

"I just know," he said simply. "You've never stopped loving me. And I've never stopped loving you."

He couldn't be more wrong. "You never loved me to begin with—"

"Yes, I did. And I love you more than anyone else on this planet. I will spend every day of the rest of my life trying to earn your trust, but you need to give me a chance first."

This still wasn't making any sense. "Cypress, I don't understand. Where is this coming from? Why have you sprung this on me a year later? I don't get it. You can have any woman you want, so why are you trying to pursue me? You already had me and threw me away. Isn't that a sign you're supposed to be with someone else?"

"No. I'm supposed to be with you." His blue eyes narrowed on mine, unflinching. He pressured me with his look, backing me into an invisible corner. "There's something I need to show you. It's gonna come as a shock. It's gonna be difficult to understand. But I want you to know we'll get through it together."

Now I really was scared. "What are you talking about?"

"Come on." He walked to his front door and opened it.

I stayed on the porch, unsure if I wanted to cross that threshold.

"You need to see it. Follow me." He walked inside his house and flipped on all the lights.

I followed him, surveying his house. The hardwood floors were deep brown, and the walls were a light gray color. He had white couches in the living room with paintings of landscapes on the wall. The furniture didn't suit him, so I assumed a designer had done it for him.

"What is it?" I asked, my voice shaking.

"Here." He grabbed a picture frame off one of the tables and sat down.

I sat beside him and looked down at the picture he was holding. It was a large eight-by-ten frame, and inside was a picture of him in a three-piece suit. His hair was styled elegantly, and he wore a charming smile.

But there was someone else in the picture.

A brunette in a wedding dress. She had green eyes just like me, the same brown hair...we looked identical. "I...I don't understand."

He took my hand, and I didn't pull away. "That's you and me in the photo. We've been married for two years."

I think I would remember something like that. "What?"

He set the picture on the table. "Eighteen months ago, you were in an accident. You were walking home from work in the dark, and a driver had a stroke and didn't see you. They hit you at twenty-five miles an hour, and you fell to the ground and hit your head on the sidewalk. You blacked out, and when you regained consciousness, you reverted back to three years in the past. Every morning after that, you did the exact same thing. Your last memory of me is when we broke up outside your place. You kicked me out and said you never wanted to see me again. So you don't remember anything that's happened ever since."

His words sank into me, but I couldn't absorb them. I couldn't believe this fantastical tale. I married the man who broke my heart? I gave him another chance when he didn't deserve it? "Then why do I remember you now?"

"I think it's because you hit your head again. It must have rewired something in your brain. That's why I'm telling you this. There's so much that's changed, and I need you to understand what's going on."

"That means...Rose and Lily are..."

"Five and seven," he answered. "Yeah. After you and I got married, we opened a few restaurants with Amelia, Blade, and Ace. We've been running them ever since."

Amelia, Blade, and Ace hated Cypress. How did they ever forgive him for what he did to me?

"Amelia and Evan got a divorce," he said quietly. "He left her for another woman...who was eighteen. They've been apart for over a year now."

That would explain the weight loss and absent wedding ring. "Amy...no."

He kept his hand on mine. "I bought the house next door so I could keep an eye on you, make sure you're okay."

"So...I've been seeing you every single day?"

He nodded. "Yeah."

"And what happens? Do I scream at you every time?"

"Not every time," he answered. "Sometimes you have good days, and you are calm."

I couldn't believe I'd ever be calm seeing him next door to me. "I...I just don't understand why I would have ever given you another chance. That doesn't sound like me."

"I was pretty persistent."

"Why?"

He brushed his thumb along my knuckles. "In the time we were apart, I knew I'd made the biggest mistake of my life. No woman ever compared to you. I knew I'd lost the woman I was supposed to spend the rest of my life with. As time went on, it didn't get any easier. So I chased you until you finally gave me another chance."

"I'm surprised I ever did..."

"Like I said, I was persistent." He continued to brush

his thumb over my skin, lightly caressing me. "I know this is a lot to take in. I understand you're probably confused and upset. But I'm here. We'll get through this together. I'll tell you everything you've missed. We'll work on our marriage and get it back to where it was before. I know we can do it."

Work on our marriage? That was the last thing on my mind. "Cypress…I don't know you. It's been a year since I last spoke to you. I don't feel that way about you…I've moved on. I can't be married to you when I don't even love you."

He cringed when he heard all of that. "You do love me. I know you do."

"If I did, I would say it. But I don't."

"I'll prove it to you. We'll take it slow. Eventually, we'll work it out."

I pulled my hand away. "I don't want to work it out, Cypress." I rose to my feet so I could have some space. "I'm sorry for being so harsh, but…I'm not in the same place. I don't remember anything. And I don't want to force this when I don't want to be with you. It would be easier to get a divorce."

"We aren't getting a divorce."

"Uh, yes, we are."

He rose to his feet and stared me down. "No."

"Yes—"

"No. You're my wife, and I'm your husband." He ground his teeth together in between sentences, suppressing his rage. "I understand this whole thing is crazy. I can't even begin to understand how you feel right now. It's a lot to take in. But we are not giving up on us. I've never given up on you, even when you didn't remember me. So you sure as hell aren't giving up on me now that you're well again."

When I saw the seriousness in his eyes, I knew he wasn't going to soften his stance. He was determined to make this work, even if I couldn't understand why. "I need to see Amelia..." She was my sister, the most important person in the world to me. She'd lost her husband, and I needed to be there for her. It was far more important than having this conversation with Cypress.

He abandoned the argument. "I'll drive you."

"No, I can walk. And I want to go alone."

"Sweetheart—"

"Please call me Bree. I want to be alone with her." I walked to the door, and Dino followed me. He stood on his hind legs and placed his paws against my hip.

I looked down at him, and something dawned on me. "That's why he's so friendly to me..."

Cypress stood with his hands in his pockets and nodded. "We got him right after we got married. I have lots of pictures of the two of you when he was just a puppy. I'll show them to you later."

I patted Dino on the head before I walked out. Something about knowing I had a dog sank right into my chest. I'd always wanted a dog, and I'd had one for years without realizing it. I turned on the flashlight on my phone so I could see in the dark and started walking.

11

BREE

As soon as I knocked on the door, Amelia answered.

She must have been expecting me because she wouldn't have answered the door so quickly. That meant Cypress called her—which didn't surprise me.

She stared at me with wet eyes, the emotion heavy in her look. When she looked like that, she reminded me of Mom. She had the same facial structure, the same cheekbones. "Bree..." She pulled me into her arms and hugged me.

"Amy." I squeezed her back, feeling the tears flood down my cheeks. "I'm so sorry."

"I'm sorry too. I'm sorry you had to go through this."

We cried together in the hallway, holding each other as we mourned for everything we'd both lost. Amelia was the first one to pull away, and she dabbed at the corners of her eyes with her fingertips. "Can I get you anything?"

"No." There was nothing in the world I wanted right then. All I wanted was my sister.

We took a seat at the kitchen table together, and I

reached out my hand and grabbed hers. "I'm so sorry about Evan…"

The tears were still in her eyes. "It was hard…still is hard."

"That fucking asshole. I can't believe he did that to you. I swear to god—"

"I know you're angry. I was livid too. But he's the father of my children, and I try to accept it. It's easier that way…"

I squeezed her hand. "I wish I had been there for you."

"I know you do. Cypress and the guys took care of me. Without them, I wouldn't have made it through. They're very sweet."

I was surprised Cypress was so involved with my sister's well-being, but I didn't make a comment on it.

"I'm so glad you're back. You call me every single day as soon as you see Cypress next door…and we have the same conversation over and over."

"Every day?" I whispered.

She nodded. "Every day."

"And I say the same thing?"

"Sometimes you're really angry. Sometimes you're just surprised. It changes on a daily basis."

"Wow…" I was surprised my opinion could change so much based on my mood. "Cypress told me everything… that we're married."

She sniffed before she nodded. "He told me you didn't take it very well."

"How else am I supposed to take it? When he cheated on me, I hated him. I wanted nothing to do with him. And then I married him? What the hell was I thinking?"

Amelia released a quiet chuckle. "Well, Cypress is very handsome and charming. But you already knew that."

"He's not charming enough."

"I know this is hard, but he really is a good guy."

"Amelia, you stormed into his apartment and punched him in the face. You hated him more than I did."

"I did," she said with a nod. "He hurt my little sister. He deserved it. But in time, I forgave him. He proved to me that he changed and became a good man. It took him a long time, but he did it. Blade and Ace didn't like him either for a lengthy period. Now we're all family."

I still couldn't believe it. "I can't believe I don't remember any of this..."

"Don't be too hard on yourself. It's not your fault."

"How did Cypress get me back? What did he say?"

She shrugged. "Honestly, I don't know the specifics. I just know he pursued you until you finally gave him a date. And then after that date, he asked for more...and then you started hooking up. You didn't tell me or the guys about that part. And then one day, you were finally back together. I think you dated for about six months before you became serious."

I shook my head in disbelief. "I'm still shocked. After what he did...I can't see me doing that."

"He's a smooth talker," she said with a smile.

"He told me we could work on our marriage and take it slow...but I don't want to do that. I asked for a divorce, and he said no."

Her smile fell. "Why won't you give it a chance?"

"Because I don't love him, Amelia. I'm over him. My last conversation with him was when I threw all his shit in the hallway and told him to never come near me again. Maybe Cypress put the moves on me and somehow convinced me to be with him. Maybe I was happy with him. Maybe I loved being married to him. But I don't feel that way now. Why should I make a marriage work when I don't even like the guy?"

"You loved being married to him," she whispered. "I've never known two people more in love."

"What?" I asked incredulously. "Seriously?"

She nodded.

"Me and Cypress?"

She nodded again.

"King of the manwhores?"

"Yes, Bree. I'm telling you, he changed for you. He really got his act together and became the man you deserved. You can always ask Blade and Ace if you don't believe me, but as your sister, I wouldn't lie to you about this. I might lie and say you don't look fat in a dress when you do, but I wouldn't lie about this. You two were so happy it made me sick." She smiled at me across the table.

I stared at our joined hands and still couldn't picture any of that being true. I loved that man once before, but the second I caught Vanessa on his lap, all those emotions faded away. How did I sleep with him without thinking about the fact that Vanessa had been there first? "I don't know what to say…"

"Cypress has taken care of me since Evan left. He babysits the girls when I'm overwhelmed, he comes out and takes care of the yardwork, brings groceries by when I don't have time to do it myself…and he's been there for me as a friend. He took your place because he knew how much it would have meant to you."

I bowed my head, touched by what she said.

"I know it's not my place, but I think you should give Cypress a chance."

"But—"

"Just think about it, okay? Don't shut it down

right away."

I closed my mouth again, knowing I needed to accept my sister's point of view. "Who's the other woman?"

"Evan's new wife?" she whispered.

I nodded.

"Her name is Jasmine. She's nineteen or so. They live in Monterey."

"How did he meet her?"

"She was out with her friends around here, and he ran into her. The rest is history."

"So...he just left?"

She nodded. "Said he'd fallen in love with someone else and asked for a divorce. It all happened really quickly."

"Did you have any idea?"

She shook her head. "When I look back on it now, there was some suspicious stuff. But at the time, I didn't think my husband would ever do that to me, so I was never paranoid about it."

God, I felt terrible for her. "What does she do?"

"She's a student at the college. He supports her."

"How is he with the girls?"

Amelia's eyes welled up with tears again. "Hardly sees them anymore. It's like he stopped caring." She covered her mouth to stifle a sob. "That's the worst part... It's like he wants nothing to do with them."

"Amelia..." I scooted my chair closer to hers and wrapped my arms around her. I listened to her sob against my shoulder.

"He doesn't give me child support, says I don't need it."

What a fucking asshole.

"I ask him to pick up the girls for the weekend, and he doesn't text back. He just wants to be young again...with a woman ten years younger than him. I gave birth to his children, and he just tossed me aside..."

I squeezed her harder. "I'm so sorry..." I didn't know what else to say to comfort her. It was devastating. It was worse than what Cypress had done to me. Evan turned his back on his entire family just because a younger woman wanted him. It was absolutely sickening.

"I know you are."

"You'll get through it. I know you will."

Amelia pulled away and wiped her eyes with a tissue. "I've already come a long way. He's been gone for a year, and I have gotten back into a routine. But when the girls ask for him, that never gets easier."

"He's gonna come back. He's gonna realize he made a huge mistake and come crawling on his hands and knees. I can promise you that."

"I hope he does...but I hope it's to be a better father to the girls. Because I would never want to be his wife again. I gave him everything, and he threw it all away."

It was exactly how I felt about Cypress. "He'll come back. The girls will have him back." I had so much faith in it because Amelia was not only beautiful, but smart and funny. She was a serious catch. When we were in school, she was always classified as the pretty sister. That was always fine with me because it was the truth.

"I hope so... I really do."

When I woke up the next morning, it was overcast, cold, and drizzly. I didn't mind the weather on days like this. I usually made a fire and read on the couch, enjoying the warmth of my cottage with a blanket over my lap.

But I needed to go to work and see Blade and Ace. I was excited to see them and hear about their lives. And I was certain they would be happy to see me too.

As soon as I stepped outside, Cypress emerged from his house.

"Are you watching me?"

"No. Are you watching me?"

I rolled my eyes and walked to the street.

He did the same.

When we were close to each other, that's when I noticed the black wedding band he wore on his finger. It made me uncomfortable, so I looked away.

Cypress walked up to me, wearing a gray hoodie and dark jeans. His dark brown hair contrasted against his fair skin, and his jaw was covered with a light amount of stubble. I remembered how thick his beard would get when he didn't shave for a week. I would rub my fingers against it and feel how coarse it was. "How are you doing?"

"I'm okay. I was at Amelia's late last night...she told me about Evan."

He sighed and looked down the road. "Yeah...it was rough. But I went to his place and gave him a mean black eye. He had the bruise for two weeks."

I immediately smiled in satisfaction. "Thank you."

"She's my sister too."

My smile dropped immediately. "Well, I'm going to work. I want to see Blade and Ace."

"Sounds like a good idea. They can't wait to see you." He started walking with me, his powerful arms swinging by his sides.

"So...how does this work? We all own the restaurants?"

"Yeah. We split the profits evenly."

"And we hop from restaurant to restaurant?"

"We all have our main zones, but we do move around a lot. The other night, one of the bartenders got sick, so I worked. Amelia works at the diner a lot because she's up early after she drops off the kids. The café is the easiest one, and Blade and I check in a lot. Ace mainly handles Olives. It's chaotic, but we make it work."

"What made you guys decide to do this?"

"It was your idea, actually. You said you wanted to expand but didn't have the manpower. I wanted to open a restaurant too, so we all worked together to make it happen. And every restaurant is successful...because of you."

"And you guys carried on while I was gone?"

"Well, you were never really gone. You already owned the café before the other restaurants, so you go in there and help out a bit. Whenever I'm there, I just sneak out the back so you don't see me."

"Oh..."

"We have our morning meetings at Amelia's Place. So that's where we'll head."

"Her apartment?"

"No, that's the name of the diner. She thought it was cute."

"It is cute."

We walked to the restaurant on Mission. When I looked through the window, I saw all the customers enjoying their coffee and breakfast. There was a line outside to get in even though it was the middle of the week.

We took the stairs to the second level and entered a large office space with several wooden desks. A banner hung from the ceiling that said, "Welcome Back, Bree!" Blade hopped out of his chair and ran to me first. He hugged me and picked me up before he spun me around. "There she is."

My arms hooked around his neck as I felt him lift me off the ground. "Oh my god."

He set me down then gave me another hug. "You have no idea how happy I am."

"I'm happy too...really happy."

Ace came next and gave me a bear hug. "Our genius entrepreneur is back. It was never the same without you."

"Thanks, Ace. I missed you. Both of you." I hadn't known what was going on when my mind was lost, but now that I was aware of what happened, I realized I had missed out on years of their lives. "I want to know everything I missed. What's going on with you?"

"Honestly, the last few years have been pretty boring," Blade said. "We pretty much just work all the time."

"It's true," Ace said as he shook his head. "We're so lame."

"Shut up, you guys aren't lame," I said with a laugh.

"Well, we've been lame without our boss to guide us," Blade said.

"Are you guys seeing anybody?" I took a seat at one of the desks, and they pulled up chairs so we could talk.

"Well, I was seeing this girl a few months ago, but it didn't go anywhere," Blade said. "I'm back on the market. If you know of anyone, let me know." He winked.

"I'm dating a woman named Lady." Ace had jet-black hair that was cropped short. He was muscular, looking like a Navy SEAL more than a restaurant owner. His arms were so big it didn't seem like they could fit inside his t-shirt. "Actually, just had my first threesome the other night."

"Whoa." I gave him a high five. "How'd it go?"

"Pretty good," Ace said. "Cypress gave me some advice that really helped."

"Of course he did…" All Cypress knew how to do was fuck.

Ace adopted a guilty look, like he regretted mentioning Cypress at all. "Anyway…it was pretty hot."

"Are you gonna do it again?" I asked.

"Depends on if Lady is cool with it," Ace said. "And I hope she is because it was awesome."

"I need to find a woman who's down for a threesome," Blade said. "Every woman I meet wants the regular committed missionary package."

"There are worse packages," I said. "I personally like that package."

"Then you need to experiment more," Ace said with a laugh.

"You guys know I'm too boring for that. I like one man, and I like having him all to myself." Maybe I was a hopeless romantic, but I knew what I wanted. "So, you guys wanna catch me up on the businesses?" I had more to say about Cypress, but since he was standing in the room, I decided to wait until I was alone with them.

"Absolutely." Blade clapped his hands. "Let's get to it."

I NEVER GOT A CHANCE TO ASK BLADE AND ACE ANYTHING because Cypress was there the whole time. But he couldn't be around all the time, so I would get my chance eventually. We walked home together, and I couldn't get around that since we were next-door neighbors.

Cypress stuck to talk about the restaurants, going over extra things with me as we headed back home. I was glad he didn't mention our relationship because I really didn't have anything to say about it right now.

I still couldn't believe we were married.

Married.

When we reached my house, he didn't go up the steps. "Have a good night. You know where to find me if you need me."

"Thanks, Cypress." I wanted a divorce, but I knew I had to forge a friendship with Cypress. He was legally tied up in the business, so it wasn't like I would ever be able to get rid of him. Maybe in time we could have what I had with Blade and Ace.

"No problem."

I turned around to walk up the stairs.

"Will you have dinner with me tomorrow night? You can come to my place. I'm a great cook."

I stopped at the top stair and looked down at him. "I told you how I felt about this."

"And I'm disregarding it because you aren't even trying."

My temper flared. "I don't have to try anything. I don't owe you anything, Cypress."

"The state of California disagrees."

I narrowed my eyes. "Why would you even want to work on a relationship with someone who doesn't remember anything? With someone who thinks you're a cheater and a liar?"

"Simple. Because I love you."

My eyes softened when I wished they wouldn't. "Cypress...I'm not trying to be mean. I don't want to hurt you. But I don't see this working."

"Because you aren't trying."

"I don't know why I gave you another chance in the first place."

"Simple. Because you love me."

I crossed my arms over my chest. "Amelia told me you were there for her when I couldn't be. I really appreciate that."

"You don't need to thank me for that. She's my family too."

"But that doesn't change anything. I don't know why you lived next door to me for eighteen months. What did you think was gonna happen?"

He shrugged. "I hoped someday you would come back to me. And if you didn't…I still wanted to take care of you. In sickness and in health, that's what we promised to each other. I was committed to you even when you had no idea what was going on. I think I deserve a chance, Bree."

"You expect me to believe that?" I asked incredulously. "That you kept it in your pants for eighteen months while you didn't get any action from your wife?"

"I got plenty of action from you." With broad shoulders and a powerful frame, he still looked taller than me even when I was on the top step.

"Did not."

"Did too. You can ask Amelia and the guys."

"You managed to get me in bed within one day? After everything you did?"

"Yep." He wore a smug look. "And no, I was never with anyone else. You're the only woman I want, Bree. Even if you don't want me right now, I'm not gonna go away. I'm not gonna let this go without a fight. I kept my end of the deal, and now you need to keep yours."

"I don't have to do anything."

"Yes, you do."

"I can get a divorce without your signature. You don't have anything over me."

"I never said I did. But you need to honor what we had. You can't throw it away. If you just give me a chance, we can make it come back."

"We can't."

"With that attitude, we can't."

"Cypress." I gave him a firm look. "I'm not gonna change my mind. I'm sorry that you wasted your time waiting around for me. I'm sorry you took care of me instead of just leaving. But I don't feel anything for you. I don't trust you. You'll always be the man who broke my heart. That's it."

"If that were the case, then why did you sleep with me?"

I stomped my foot. "How should I know? I don't even remember those nights, so how can I answer you?"

"It's easy. You still love me. Despite what I did, you still loved me. That's why you gave me another chance. And you're gonna give me another chance now. I'll earn your trust. I'll prove myself to you. I'll make you fall in love with me all over again. But I need you to give me that chance first."

No way in hell. I didn't see him as the man I wanted to spend the rest of my life with. I saw him as the cheating playboy who ripped out my heart and stomped on it. After what he put me through, I deserved better.

I turned around and walked to my front door, exhausted by the conversation.

"I'll get you back, sweetheart. Trust me."

I got the door open and turned around before I walked inside. "Good luck."

12

Bree

Amelia was downstairs working in the diner, and Cypress was manning the café on Ocean, so that left me alone with Ace and Blade.

Blade had his feet on the desk, his gray Keds on display. With his hands behind his head, he looked out the window to the small apartment complex next door. "I wonder what it's like to live in town. Is it loud all the time?"

"I doubt it's quiet." Ace worked on his laptop, doing the books for each restaurant separately. "And since most places close at nine, kinda sucks. You can't just walk down the street and get a six-pack of beer. You'd have to drive to the Crossroads in Carmel Valley."

I was trying to get my life back on track, but that wasn't such a simple thing to accomplish. So much time had passed, and I'd missed everything. The only business I remembered was the Hippopotamus Café. Now I was learning three new ones.

Blade turned his gaze on me. "You doing okay, Bree?"

"Yeah, I'm fine." My thoughts had wandered off. "Just thinking…"

Ace shut his laptop. "You know you can talk to us. We don't have vaginas, but we can be pretty girly sometimes."

"Really girly," Blade repeated. "Working with Amelia all the time and helping out with the girls has really softened us."

I smiled, appreciating their niceness. "It's just hard to understand everything. I still can't believe I married Cypress. What the hell was I thinking?"

Blade shrugged. "He's definitely a nice piece of eye candy."

Ace narrowed his eyes at him. "Dude, what's wrong with you?"

"What?" Blade asked defensively. "He is. You don't need to be gay to figure that out."

Ace shook his head. "Weirdo…"

"Are you saying you think he's ugly?" Blade challenged.

"No," Ace countered. "I'm not saying anything about him."

"So you're totally oblivious to people who are attractive and not attractive? You can't tell the difference?"

This argument could go on for a while. "Okay, Cypress is hot. I definitely agree with you on that. That's why I asked him out in the first place. But he doesn't offer anything else."

"I don't know about that," Ace said. "He's smart, loyal, hardworking… I have nothing but good things to say about that guy."

"Yeah," Blade added. "He's my best friend."

"Hey." Ace threw up his arms. "What about me?"

"What?" Blade asked. "I can't have more than one best friend?"

Ace slowly lowered his arms. "Wouldn't kill you to say it once in a while..."

As strange as they were, I'd missed this so much. "Last thing I remember, you guys wanted to kill Cypress."

"Of course we did." Blade took his feet off the desk and lowered them to the floor. "We hated that guy. When you started seeing him again, we weren't happy about it."

"Gave him a lot of shit." Ace leaned back in his chair and crossed his arms over his chest. "Made a lot of threats. But that never stopped him."

"When did you start liking him?" I asked.

"When he proved that he had changed," Blade answered. "He always hung out with us, even when we ignored him. He kept trying to be with you, even when you said no. But after a few months, we noticed how happy you were. So we finally let it go. As time went on, he seemed different. Never saw him even look at another woman. And the entire time you lost your memory, I still never saw him look at another woman."

"Me neither," Ace said. "We didn't have eyes on him every second of the day, but I'm pretty sure he never hooked up with someone else. He wore his wedding ring anytime he was out, and when women made passes at him, he always said he was married."

I tried not to be touched by that, not when he'd already cheated on me once. I didn't want to soften for him because I didn't want to be one of those women who made the mistake of giving their cheating ex another chance. It was always a bad decision.

"You aren't giving him the time of day?" Blade asked.

"No," I answered. "He said we need to work on our

relationship, but there is no relationship as far as I'm concerned. I want a divorce, but he says he's not gonna let that happen."

"I remember you felt this exact same way when he first asked you out," Ace said. "He asked you out ten different times, and you always said no. Hated him then like you do right now."

"I remember that too," Blade said. "I guess I'm not surprised. It'll take time for you to change your mind."

I cocked my head to the side in surprise. "You think I should change my mind?"

"Uh…" Blade looked at Ace, silently asking for help.

"Well…you guys were really happy," Ace added. "I mean, like movie love."

"Movie love?" I asked, unsure what that meant.

"Yeah, like soul mates and shit," Ace said. "You guys acted like you were meant to be."

I was meant to be with a cheater? "Me and Cypress?"

"Yeah," Blade answered. "It was that way for so long, it's hard for me to remember you guys weren't together at one point. It's kinda weird, actually."

My friends wouldn't lie to me, so I believed every word they said. But I couldn't wrap my mind around it.

"Don't be too hard on yourself," Blade said. "It's a lot to take in. Give it a few months. But I think you should cut Cypress some slack."

"Yeah," Ace added. "You don't have to go back to being married to him right away, but at least be nice to him. He really was the best husband in the world to you. He never gave up on you. I mean, the guy bought the house next door and took care of you every single day. That's serious commitment right there."

The guilt seeped into my skin. When my friends put it

that way, I felt bad for being so cold to him. He wasn't vindicated for what he'd done to me in the past, but he was a sweet person in the present. My entire family was defending him, and I valued their opinion more than anyone else's.

Blade stared at me as he waited for a response.

Ace propped his chin on his hand as he looked at me.

"Thanks for letting me know. I'll try to treat him better." That was all I could do right now. There was nothing they could say to make me move back in with Cypress and go back to being married. That would just be too weird.

Ace gave me a thumbs-up.

"Sounds good to me," Blade said.

As if Cypress had been listening at the door, he walked into the office. He wore dark jeans and an olive t-shirt, and his expansive chest looked strong in the fabric. There was no denying he had the perfect body. Along with that movie star face, he could get a woman on her hands and knees with a snap of a finger. No wonder why he managed to get me into bed several times over the last eighteen months.

His eyes immediately moved to mine first, acknowledging my presence before looking at the guys. The look was possessive without any effort. He looked at me like he owned me, without claiming me with words. His black wedding ring was on his left hand, exactly where it was yesterday.

I wondered where my ring was.

"What's up?" Cypress finally stopped staring and took a seat in one of the armchairs in the corner. The office was messy and disorganized, and natural light filtered through all the windows. Three of the walls were nothing but windows, and since we were elevated above the trees, we got a lot of light. Most of the furniture looked old, like it had already been there when we leased the place.

"Nothing," Blade answered. "Just doing some bookkeeping. You know, snooze fest."

"Actually, I'm the one doing the bookkeeping," Ace said. "You're doing jack shit."

Blade crumpled up a piece of paper and chucked it at his face.

Ace easily maneuvered out of the way and got comfortable again. "Don't plan to play for the major leagues…or even the minor leagues."

"I'm sure if I hit you with my fist, I wouldn't miss this time," Blade threatened.

"Shh," I finally said. "We've still got the rest of the day. Pace yourselves."

Ace stuffed his laptop into his desk and shut the drawer. "I should get down to Olives. The lunch rush is about to hit." He got out of his chair, dressed in slacks and a collared shirt. "One of my bartenders called in sick tonight. Do you think you can cover, Cypress?"

"Yeah, I'll be there," Cypress answered.

I couldn't picture Cypress bartending, but with a beautiful face like that, he probably did a great job. The drinks could taste like shit, but it wouldn't matter. He wouldn't get a single complaint.

"We could use another waitress tonight," Ace added, looking at me.

The Hippopotamus Café closed at five, so I didn't usually have anything to do in the evenings. And since I owned four restaurants, I had to pull my weight. If Ace was working the lunch hour, Amelia was doing the morning rush, and Cypress was bartending, I'd look pretty lazy if I said no. "Sure. I need some practice anyway. It's been a while." Well, it really hadn't been a while. But this was a new restaurant and a new atmosphere.

"Cool," Ace said. "I'm sure Cypress can give you the rundown while you're there."

As much as I didn't like the arrangement, I was gonna have to get used to it. We were business partners, after all.

Cypress knocked on my door at five in the evening. "You ready for work?" He was in black jeans and a black t-shirt. With pretty blue eyes and a hard jaw, he could easily be a star in a movie. At least three women would undoubtedly make a pass at him tonight—even if he was wearing his ring.

"Yeah. Is this okay?" I was in a tight black dress with flat sandals.

"Yeah. You look great."

Cypress didn't mention our relationship or anything else serious as we walked to work. He just talked about the restaurant and the way the orders ran. "The bar is pretty small, but there's usually about a dozen people waiting for a table, so it can get crowded."

"What kind of liquor do we have?"

"Everything under the sun. But we have an extensive wine category."

"Cool."

"Do you have any questions?" The restaurant had a wooden door and large windows that were fingerprint-free. Every table was full, and Mediterranean-inspired tablecloths were on each one, a mixture of gold, orange, and red.

"No. But if I do, I'll let you know."

We walked inside, and Cypress greeted the host, a cute woman with curly brown hair. She smiled wide when she saw him, a little overly enthused to see her boss.

"I don't think you've met Bree," he said as he placed his hand in the center of my back. "She's also an owner. She's been out of town for a while, so she's getting back into the swing of things."

"Such a pleasure to meet you." She shook my hand. "I'm Albany."

"Nice to meet you too."

Cypress stepped closer to me. "She's also my wife."

The blood drained from my face, but I didn't correct him. Technically, it was true. He must have told people that I existed, and most people probably knew exactly who I was. But it was still hard to swallow.

"Oh..." She smiled again, but this time, it was clearly fake. "That's wonderful." Another couple walked inside, and she took their name down since there was a wait.

I wanted to tell Cypress to stop telling people we were together, but I really couldn't stop him. If people already knew, it wasn't like it was brand-new information.

Cypress guided me to the back, his hand still on my lower back.

I wanted to push it away, but I didn't want to make a scene in public. Customers and employees were watching. Didn't want them to think we were unhinged. Cypress explained the different stations and where the orders went. He handed me a pen and paper. "If you need anything, I'm right at the bar."

"Alright. Thanks."

He looked down at me like he was concerned. His handsome face had a harder expression than usual.

"I'll be fine."

He finally walked out of the kitchen and to the bar.

I waited on the tables, and sometimes I lost my footing. I had a table of eight people, and that was a little overwhelming. It took me a few hours before I finally got back into my groove. Soon, I managed the tables like a pro, getting refills and memorizing orders without having to write them down.

When I glanced over at the bar, Cypress looked like he was in his element. He wore a handsome smile as he talked to a group of three pretty women. He had a fifty sitting on the counter, a generous and unnecessary tip.

I didn't care, so I stopped watching him.

By the end of the night, the restaurant was a mess, so we all worked together to take care of the tablecloths, tables, and chairs, and swept the floor that was covered with pieces of gyros and rice.

Cypress took care of all the glasses and locked up the expensive booze. He counted his tip money at the counter when he was finished. There must have been hundreds of dollars.

"What are you gonna buy Dino?" I took off my apron and set it on the counter.

He chuckled. "I already spoil that dog. I'm not buying him shit. How'd you do?"

"I got a lot more tips than I usually do at the café, that's for sure." That was because I didn't get any tips at all.

"Then what are you gonna buy Dino?"

"I don't know. Does he need any toys?"

Cypress laughed. "You should come over and see his toy box. It's ridiculous."

Even though I didn't remember Dino, I was already affectionate toward him. He was a sweet dog, and my heart melted every time I looked at him. I felt a connection to him because he still remembered me and loved me even though I didn't remember him. It comforted me somehow.

"How did you feel tonight?"

"Pretty good. A little stressful, though."

"You'll get the hang of it."

"Well, I hope I don't have to waitress too often. I prefer the café."

"You'll hop around. Amelia really likes Amelia's Place. Much different atmosphere."

"Yeah, I noticed when I walked by this morning."

He placed the money in his wallet and returned it to his pocket. "Ready to go?"

"Sure."

We left the restaurant and locked up before we walked back to the house. We lit up the flashlights on our phones so we could see where we were going in the darkness.

"Those girls seemed to like you." I didn't know what possessed me to make the comment. It just came out.

"What girls?"

"The ones who left you a fifty dollar tip."

He grinned. "For not liking me very much, you sure seem to be jealous."

"Not jealous. I was gonna tell you that if we just get divorced, you'll be free to do whatever you want."

His smile fell instantly. "I don't want anyone else, Bree. It's not an act. It's the truth."

I kept my eyes on the road, watching my step so I didn't get my foot stuck in a crack.

"Besides, they had nothing on you, sweetheart."

He really was different. "Where was this when we were together the first time?"

The best response he had was a shrug. "I was an idiot back then. I was in college... I was stupid."

"It's not like you were a child. You were a grown man in every capacity."

"I'm not making excuses," he said calmly. "I'm just telling you I was different back then. I didn't treat you the way you deserved. I made a really bad decision that I've always regretted. After losing you, it made me realize I needed to get my shit together because I had the most incredible woman in the world, and I lost her. That was the moment I changed, the moment I became the man you deserved."

"What happened that night, anyway?" I hadn't asked because there'd never been an opportunity. I was too busy screaming and throwing shit at him to have a real conversation.

"With Vanessa?"

"Yeah."

After a long pause, he answered. "Does it matter?"

"Yes."

He sighed under his breath. "She came over and dropped off some beer for my birthday. I thought the gesture was innocent. Didn't see any harm from taking it. Then she came inside and got on her knees... I don't need to give you any more specifics. I got lost in the moment and didn't think at all."

"So, were you still in love with her?"

"Not at all."

"Was I not satisfying you?"

"Of course you were. But I was a stupid asshole who was thinking with his dick. If you expect me to provide some profound reason for my behavior, you won't get it. I was a fucking dick. That's it. I don't blame you for leaving me. I would have judged you if you'd stayed."

At least he was honest. "Did you ever get back together with her?"

"No. We didn't hook up again after that night."

"Why not?"

"I don't know. Whenever I thought about her, I thought about how much I hurt you. Killed any arousal I had."

"Then you came back to me a year later?"

"Yeah." He turned right, and we walked downhill. "I dated a few women, had a few one-night stands, but I was never happy. I kept thinking about you, remembering how funny you were and all the good times we had. At some point, I knew I'd made the worst mistake of my life. I wanted another chance. I wanted to be what you deserved. That's when I changed. That's when I became someone you deserved. So I worked my ass off to prove myself to you. Finally, one day, you went on a date with me. The rest is history."

"I wish I remembered it."

"That makes two of us."

We turned on Casanova and approached our houses.

"I'm willing to do it all over again," he whispered. "Because what we had was pretty incredible. It's hard to believe, but it's true."

My anger toward him softened because I heard the

sincerity in his voice. I didn't want to be cold to him anymore. He had been patient with me for a long time and didn't deserve such harshness. "My family has nothing but good things to say about you." I stopped in front of his house, standing in the darkness under the cypress tree.

"It took me a long time to earn their trust back. It didn't happen overnight."

"I know...they consider you family now."

He nodded, and hope emerged in his eyes. "Does that mean you'll work on this with me? We can take it slow. We can date each other, get to know one another all over again, and then maybe...we can move in together."

"Cypress...I don't know."

He bowed his head and sighed in disappointment.

"My feelings haven't changed. I know that's frustrating, but you must understand."

"No, I do," he said quietly. "I really do."

"We're business partners, and you're obviously a part of my life now, so I want to make something work. I'd definitely like to be friends. Maybe we can be really close friends. But that's all I can give you. When I look at you, I don't see a devoted and committed husband. I see the guy who broke my heart."

He didn't lift his head again. "I get it, sweetheart. But if you give it some time, you'll feel differently. I promise. Just give me a chance. That's all I'm asking."

"I still want a divorce..."

He lifted his head, sadness in his eyes.

"I want to be free. If I meet someone else, I don't want to be tied down to you."

"You aren't gonna meet someone else."

"You don't know that—"

"I'm not gonna let that happen," he said with a clenched jaw. "I've been through hell living next door to the woman I love without being able to tell her who the fuck I am. I'm not letting you go, sweetheart. I'm sorry to be so aggressive, but you're forcing my hand."

"You can't control me."

"I'm not trying to. I've offered to be patient with you. I've offered to completely start over with you. Anything you want, I'll give it to you. But I want a fair chance."

"Even if I give you a chance, I still want a divorce."

"Why?" he demanded.

"Because if we ever do get back together, I want to experience all of that again. I want to be proposed to. I want a wedding. I don't want to see my memories in pictures…I want to live it myself."

He moved closer to me and placed his hands on my hips. "I guess I can understand that. But I still want you to give me a chance."

"I…I don't know. Can we try being friends first?"

"So that means you'll keep an open mind about it?"

I still couldn't get over the fact that he'd cheated on me. I wasn't sure why I gave him another chance to begin with. "I guess…"

"That's all I ask." He dug his fingers into my sides, gripping me tighter than he did before. He moved in closer, just as he had the other day when he'd kissed me.

I held my breath, fearing that was next on the agenda.

"I was hoping you could do something for me."

"What is it?"

He looked at my lips for a long time before he looked me in the eye. "The thing I miss most about us being together…is just being together. Whenever I get you in bed, I have to leave before you wake up the next morning.

Whenever we see each other, you're usually telling me how much you hate me. I just...want to hold you. Is it okay if I hold you?"

I'd been expecting a very different request. It was sweet, so I couldn't deny him. After everything he'd done for me, a hug wasn't too much to ask for. "Yeah."

He pulled me into his chest and circled his arms completely around me, drawing me into his body with the strength of his core. Even though he was a foot taller than me, he buried his face in my neck and released the air he was holding in his lungs.

My arms circled his neck, and I closed my eyes. I could feel his heart beating against my skin, slow and steady. He smelled like pine needles and booze from working at the restaurant all night. The fabric of his shirt was exquisitely soft, and I imagined how it would feel to wear one of his shirts to bed.

The street was dead quiet. There weren't any cars at this time of night, and there weren't any pedestrians either since everything was closed after about nine. It was just the two of us under the cypress tree in his front yard.

The hug lasted for a long time, stretching into minutes. His breathing evened with every passing minute, growing deeper and steadier. His heart beat at the same pace, still slow and powerful. His lips remained against my neck, but he didn't kiss me. Sometimes they moved slightly, and they brushed against me, sticking to my warm skin.

It felt nice.

It reminded me of the way he used to hold me after we'd made love in my bed. He would snuggle with me all night, his powerful body acting as a heater when the cold air came in through an open window I forgot to close.

After nearly thirty minutes of standing in the driveway, he pulled away and looked at me. Now he didn't wear an expression of intensity. Instead, it was a look of vulnerability. His hands slowly slid down my waist until they found my hips. He leaned in and pressed a kiss to my forehead, the embrace lasting for a long time. "Good night..." He finally turned away and let me go, not looking back as he walked into his house and shut the door.

It took me a moment to process what had just happened, and more importantly, how I felt about it. When he held me like that, I could understand why I softened for him. I could see why I changed my mind about him. Being the center of his universe, the object of his focus, felt really nice.

I finally shook it off and walked into my house, feeling a little differently toward him than I had that morning.

13

Amelia

I grabbed the plates of the pecan pancakes combo and the eggs Benedict and brought it to the table. "Anything else? More coffee?" I placed the check on the table then walked to the check-in counter. "Well, I'm done for the day." I untied my apron and hung it up on the hanger.

Cypress took care of the receipts and the cash in the register. "Me too. I'm tired."

"Tired because something happened last night...?"

He separated the wads of money into piles. A grin stretched his face. "Well, I got a hug."

"You're smiling over a hug?"

"It was a long hug. I haven't hugged my wife in years, so it was pretty amazing."

My eyes softened, and my heart ached. I wish Evan had loved me that way. When I thought back on our marriage, I wondered if he ever had. "Bree is coming over tonight to spend time with the girls."

"I have to work anyway, so I guess that's fine. Feel her out for me, will ya?"

"Sure."

"I asked for another chance, but she said she still wants a divorce. But at least she said she would keep an open mind...that we could be friends."

"You aren't really going to divorce her, right?"

"I'm stalling as long as I can." He placed rubber bands around the rolls of cash and dropped them into the leather bag. "I'm really gonna have to crank up the charm."

"How do you plan to do that?"

"Do push-ups and sit-ups without my shirt on."

I laughed because I thought he was joking.

"I'm being serious. Works pretty well."

"And you just leave all your windows open and hope she looks?"

"Oh, she'll look. I know my wife. She's kinda a slut when it comes to me." He zipped the bag and winked at me.

I chuckled. "I hope you're right."

"I'm gonna deposit this then head over to Olives. See you later."

"Bye." I watched him walk out before I started cleaning up the diner. There were still a few customers taking their time at the tables, but I cleaned up around them.

BREE WALKED IN THE DOOR AFTER FIVE. SHE WAS IN A PAIR of jeans and a dark green sweater. The second she was inside, she unzipped it and hung it on the coat rack. Instead of smiling or even saying hi to me, she looked nervous.

"They remember you." I placed my hand on her back. "Don't worry about it."

"But it's been years."

"Like I'd ever let them forget about their aunt. I talk about you all the time. They're in the living room."

Bree walked into the living room where the girls were playing. When they recognized her, they both jumped to their feet and hugged her at the exact same time. "Aunt Bree!" Rose squealed.

Bree kneeled down and hugged them, and within seconds, she started to cry. "I missed you…"

"We missed you too," Lily whispered.

I walked into the kitchen to give Bree some privacy. Besides, I was starting to cry, and I'd already cried enough these past two weeks.

My phone was sitting on the kitchen counter, and it lit up with a text message from Ace. *I'm coming by with groceries right now. Cypress told me to pick up a few things.*

The second I realized he was coming, a lump moved into my throat. My heart pounded a little harder, and sweat collected on my palms. I shouldn't let the butterflies get to me, not when he didn't even know I existed sexually, but I couldn't help it. Being alone for a year didn't help matters. I wouldn't mind if we just hooked up for a one-night stand and never talked about it again.

When I walked back into the living room, Bree was coloring with the girls. She and Rose were both working on a pink dragon with a soldier sitting on its back. The TV was on with their favorite cartoon, and Bree fit right in like she used to. I sat on the couch and enjoyed a glass of wine, relieved I had a break from entertaining my kids. Bree was basically a free babysitter.

Ace knocked on the door a few minutes later.

I was in my tight jeans and a t-shirt. My hair and makeup were done, so I looked a lot better than I did when I was working at the diner. I opened the door and gave him a warm smile. "Thanks for the delivery."

"No problem." He had a large case of firewood with three brown paper bags sitting on top. It must have weighed sixty pounds, but he carried it effortlessly. He set it on the counter before moving the bags around. "Cypress was working late, so he asked me to stop by Bruno's Market before they closed."

"You didn't have to do that. I could have picked it up."

"Nonsense. I don't mind."

I loved how thick his arms were. They were like tree trunks. I could easily picture him on top of me, his tight ass working hard to thrust into me. I would love to drag my nails down his muscular back and feel his strength.

I forced myself to look away before I made myself too obvious.

"Besides, the firewood is pretty heavy."

"Huh?" I lost track of what we were talking about.

He tapped the box with his hand. "I said, the box is heavy."

"Oh…I could have managed."

He walked up to me and circled his arm around my waist, giving me a quick hug.

I almost jumped out of my skin because a hug was too sexual for me. I wanted him to press me against the counter and fuck me while my daughters had no idea what was going on in the other room.

Instead, he gave me a friendly hug and pulled away. "How's Bree doing?"

"She's bonding with the kids. It's going well."

"That's good. I knew they wouldn't forget about her. They're too smart."

I loved the way he praised my kids. It didn't seem like he wanted kids of his own right now, but I could tell he would be a good father whenever he was ready.

"You want me to get out of your hair, or is it cool if I hang around?"

There was nothing I wanted more. "Of course. You wanna beer?"

"I'll help myself." He snatched one out of the fridge and twisted the cap off. He leaned against the counter and crossed his ankles.

"So...how are things doing with Lady?"

"Good." He lowered his voice and turned to me. "Did I tell you I had a threesome the other night?"

I already didn't want to hear about Lady, so I certainly didn't want to hear about another girl in the mix. I was just waiting for the happy news that he'd gotten tired of her and moved on. But if she was willing to do frisky stuff like that, he wasn't gonna drop her anytime soon. "No..."

He grinned pompously. "Yeah, pretty crazy. My first one." He drank his beer and smiled at the same time.

I wanted to throw up.

Bree's voice interrupted our conversation. I didn't even know she'd been standing there. "Hey, Ace."

"Hey, Bree." He wrapped one arm around her and gave her a hug. "How's it going with the little ones?"

"Great," she said. "I can't believe how big they've gotten. And so smart too."

"They get that from Amelia," Ace said. "Their cuteness too."

I felt my cheeks get warm.

"I'm gonna say hi." Ace set down his beer and walked into the living room. "How are my girls?"

I stayed in the kitchen, feeling my sister stare at me without blinking.

"What?" I wiped my cheek, thinking something was on my face.

"Nothing." Her eyes remained narrowed.

It wasn't nothing. "What?" I repeated.

"I just…I thought I saw something there."

"Between me and Ace?" I asked incredulously. "He just told me he had a threesome."

"And you looked pretty devastated."

"No…just grossed out. That's all."

Unfortunately, Bree was the one person in the world who could practically read my mind. "I don't know…seemed odd."

"You're overthinking it. I'm gonna order a pizza. Do you want any?"

Bree finally let it go. "Yeah, sure. No sausage though. Yuck."

I smiled. "I remember."

ACE PUT THE GIRLS TO BED EVEN THOUGH I HADN'T ASKED him to before he came back into the living room. He grabbed his beer and took a long drink before he pulled a slice out of the box and dropped it on his plate. "Evan is the biggest piece of shit in the world…but at least he gave you those girls. They're perfect." He took an enormous bite, getting half of the pizza into his mouth instantly.

"Thank you." A lot of people told me my girls were adorable, and that was because they were. I was biased because I was their mother, but it was the truth. A part of me wished I'd never married Evan and had taken a different path, but I could never regret the beautiful gifts I got out of that marriage.

Rose and Lily.

Ace turned to Bree. "How's it going with Cypress?"

"I wouldn't say it's *going*," she said. "I'm just getting to know him all over again. We both worked at Olives last night. That was interesting."

"So you guys are working it out?" Ace assumed.

"No...I'm trying to be his friend for now," she answered. "He told me he wants to work on our relationship, but I just don't see him like that right now. It'll take a long time."

"I'm glad you're keeping an open mind about it," I said. "Cypress really is a great guy. You aren't gonna find anyone better." I felt bad for pressuring my sister when she was capable of making her own decisions, but I didn't want her to lose Cypress. He'd more than made up for the terrible mistake he made.

"Me too," Ace said. "That guy really loves you."

"So I hear," she whispered.

Ace ate another piece of pizza. "Well, thanks for the free food. I should get going." He tossed his paper plate in the garbage and walked to the front door.

I walked him out. "I'll see you in the morning."

"Yeah." He gave me a quick hug before he walked out.

I returned to the living room and was immediately a target for my sister's hot gaze. "What?"

"You have a thing for him?"

How did she pick up on that so quickly? "No. Why?"

"Because it's really obvious. You stared at him the entire time."

"I've never seen anyone eat that fast before."

"Oh, shut up." She rolled her eyes. "Blade can do laps around Ace. You were staring at him for a completely different reason, and we both know it."

Dammit.

"Amelia."

"What?" I said with a sigh.

"Am I right?"

I crossed my arms over my chest and sank into the couch. "I think you've already figured out your answer."

"I knew it." She slammed her hand down on the couch. "How long has this been going on?"

"I don't know…a few months. Don't mention anything to him."

She shot me an irritated look. "Oh, come on. Like I ever would."

"I don't know…you have a big mouth."

"You know I would never do that. Do Cypress and Blade know?"

I nodded.

"Why haven't you made a move?"

"He doesn't see me like that, unfortunately."

"He used to have a huge crush on you in high school."

"That was ten years ago," I reminded her. "Now I'm a single mom with two kids."

"And still fine as hell," she said. "Come on, are you a size two?"

"A four," I snapped. "But that's not the point."

"If you're into him, you should tell him. What's the worst that could happen?"

"He says no, and it's awkward as hell. That's what."

She shrugged. "Ace isn't like that. He wouldn't be weird about it."

"Trust me, I know when a man is into me. Ace doesn't look at me like that. He only sees a friend."

"Then give him a reason to see you in a different way."

"What am I supposed to do? Just walk up and kiss him and see what happens?"

"That'd be perfect."

I was joking. "I'm not doing that."

"Why not? Ace is the kind of guy who would love something like that. It's spontaneous. It's sexy."

"He's seeing someone."

Bree waved it off. "Whatever. She's not serious. He's having threesomes with her. She's just a piece of ass."

"It's still wrong."

"You're overthinking it. You want him, go get him."

"I'm just lonely right now. I probably only like Ace because he's nice to me."

"And he's hot as hell and built like a brick house," Bree said. "That has a lot to do with it, I'm sure."

"Forget I said anything, okay? Nothing is gonna happen."

"Whatever..." Bree got comfortable on the couch and faced the TV.

"You're the last person who should be talking about relationships, by the way."

"Why?" She propped her feet on the opposite armrest. "Because I'm married to a cheater?"

"He's not a cheater."

"I distinctly remember him fucking Vanessa in his bed. Yes, he's a cheater."

"That was, like, four years ago."

"It wasn't that long for me, remember?" She hugged a pillow to her chest and watched the TV. "I honestly don't see how Cypress and I will ever make it work. I don't see him the way the rest of you do. He's gorgeous, obviously. He's got the sexiest body in the world, duh. But the second I look at him, my heart screams in pain."

"You'll see past it eventually."

"I don't know…"

"You did the first time."

"And I'm still not sure how that happened." She grabbed the blanket off the back of the couch and draped it over herself. "Do you mind if I sleep here?"

"Sure. But I'm gonna wake you up at the crack of dawn when I get my kids ready for school."

"That's fine with me."

"Why don't you want to go home?"

She gave me a firm look. "You know exactly why."

I worked at the diner the following morning, and when the rush was over, I tossed my apron to the side and took care of the register. The rest of the employees cleaned up while I walked upstairs and headed into the office.

Ace sat at his desk while playing on his phone. "Hey. How was your morning?" He didn't look up from his phone.

"Pretty good. It was packed, like usual. I'm excited for the weekend."

"Oh yeah…" He finished what he was doing on his phone and tossed it on the table. "I was gonna ask if you could waitress tomorrow night at Olives. I'll be there too, but one of my girls called in sick this weekend. Don't have anyone to replace her."

"What about Bree and Cypress?"

"They're already working. Blade asked for the night off because he's having dinner with his parents in Monterey."

That was the one thing I hated about this business. When employees flaked, it was up to us to keep the business going. "Alright. I'll just make sure I get a sitter. Shouldn't be too hard."

"Sorry. You know I hate taking you away from the girls."

I smiled. "I know, Ace." I sat down and organized the money at my desk. "What are you doing?"

"I've been meaning to finish the bookkeeping for taxes, but since it's so goddamn boring, I've been going at a snail's pace."

"I hear ya."

"I'll get through it. I just need to stop going on social media and distracting myself."

I organized all the money into separate piles before I tossed it back into the leather pouch. "So...this thing with Lady. Is it serious?" It wasn't out of line for me to ask. We discussed everything with each other. If I were dating someone, he'd probably question me about it too.

He rubbed his chin as he considered my question, looking hot as hell in the long-sleeve black shirt he wore. He filled out his clothes well, masculine and strong. I'd love to feel those soft but manly lips against mine...and everywhere else on my body. "I don't really know. We're kinda just fooling around and talking."

So that was a definite no.

"Why?"

"Uh..." I wasn't planning on making a move. Bree put stupid thoughts into my head, but I wasn't going to act on them. "You mentioned you had a threesome, so I was just curious if she was just a fuck buddy."

"I guess. She's pretty kinky...but I like kinky." He chuckled to himself then opened the laptop.

I tried not to vomit into my throat.

The next night, I went into Olives with my hair done, my makeup heavy, and a skintight dress hugging my figure.

Bree walked up to me, also wearing a dress with her hair up. "Damn, you look pretty damn good for having two kids."

"Why, thank you." I smoothed out my dress before I tied my apron around my waist.

"Any special occasion?" she asked as she glanced at Ace. "Because I'm pretty sure you just bought that today."

"No." I swatted her wrist. "No reason."

She looked at Ace again. "He's checking you out."

"He is?" I asked with more enthusiasm than I should express.

"Oh yeah. He's coming this way..." Bree disappeared and walked into the back kitchen so I could talk to him alone.

Ace whistled under his breath. "Day-yum, you look gorgeous tonight."

I couldn't stop my cheeks from turning bright red. I knew Ace had complimented me in a friendly way, not a creepy way like some guys did, and it made me feel special. It made me feel like the other women he checked out when they walked past. I didn't feel like someone who was just his friend—but an attractive woman instead. "Thanks."

"Baby, you're gonna get so many tips." He winked then

placed his hand on my hip. He gave me a gentle squeeze before he walked away.

Bree was on the other side of the room at the bar. She locked eyes with me then gave me a thumbs-up.

I hoped I wasn't making myself as obvious to him as I was to everyone else. I got to work and waited on the tables, letting the hours go by. Ace was working as the manager that evening, so he answered the phone, ran food to the tables, and helped out with other tasks. Sometimes when he passed me, he gave me a smile that lit up the entire restaurant.

I felt my crush grow in intensity.

I walked over to the bar to get two glasses of wine for my table. "Two of the rosé."

Cypress poured them in front of me. "If your goal was to get his attention, you succeeded."

Even Cypress knew what I was doing?

He gave me a smile. "He's been checking out your ass all night."

I never thought I'd be excited about that. "Thanks." I carried the glasses to the table and tried not to look at Ace. I hadn't felt this good in a long time, felt this attractive. Toward the end of my marriage to Evan, I didn't get any affection. When he told me about his bimbo, I understood why I hadn't gotten laid in months. It was because he preferred another woman to me. That had been a major attack on my self-esteem. I hadn't fully recovered.

At the end of the night, we closed the restaurant and got to cleaning.

"Cypress and I need to take off," Bree said. "We cleaned the bar and the tables, but we need to stop by the office and check on something."

I knew exactly what she was doing.

Ace didn't figure it out. "See you tomorrow."

Bree gave me a final look before she walked out with Cypress. They turned left toward their houses instead of right, so that was a dead giveaway they were making an excuse so I could be alone with Ace.

Bree wanted me to just walk up to him and kiss him.

Like I could pull that off.

Ace wiped everything down before he walked to the desk at the entrance and finished taking care of the money along with the reservation book.

I didn't have anything else to do because I was done with all my tasks. I could just walk out and return to my kids, but I stayed put. The trees outside were wrapped with white lights, and the sidewalk was deserted. It seemed like it was just the two of us in the whole world.

I shouldn't do it. Nothing good would come of it.

But I really wanted to kiss him.

He looked so strong in that black collared shirt. It fit his hard body perfectly, his chiseled mass extending down to thin hips. He had long and toned legs, muscular thighs. Even his feet were sexy. I'd looked at them a few times on the beach.

What if I kissed him, and he pulled away? Would I damage our friendship?

But what if I kissed him, and he didn't pull away?

What if it turned into something?

It didn't seem like he thought of me in a romantic way, but Bree was right. What if I changed his mind about that?

My hands were shaking, and I was out of breath. I'd kissed many men in my day, but I'd never been so nervous. The last man I kissed was my ex-husband, who left me for someone else. My confidence was gone. If Ace rejected me, I wasn't sure I could recover.

But I had to try.

Even if we didn't turn into something romantic, anything would feel nice.

I walked toward him slowly, my heels echoing against the hardwood floor. All the lights in the back kitchen had been turned off, so it was darker in the restaurant than it usually was. No one was watching us because there wasn't a single person on the sidewalk at this time of night.

I stopped when I was just inches from him, my heart blasting right against my rib cage.

When he felt me right next to him, he straightened and looked at me, expecting me to say something.

Now I had to do it. I was closer to him than I'd ever been.

He glanced at my lips, almost as if he knew what I was going to do.

So I went for it.

I hooked my arms around his neck and kissed him, my soft lips feeling perfect against his. I slowly moved my mouth, feeling the bristles of his facial hair rub against my cheeks. Instantly, he kissed me back.

He kissed me back.

His pace matched mine, slow and steady. His kisses were purposeful, focused. He felt my mouth with his, memorizing every contour of my lips. He slid his hand into my hair, and he guided me away from the door, still kissing me.

It felt incredible.

Far better than it ever had with Evan.

He kept backing me up until we were jammed against the wall in between two tables. His massive body pressed against mine, and he explored my curves with his big hands. He started at my hips then moved up my stomach.

He glided his hands over my ribs before his fingers reached my tits. He kissed me harder as he groped them, squeezing them through my dress and bra.

It felt so good to be touched that way.

I got excited and wrapped my leg around his waist, my dress riding up and my thong exposed.

He ran his hand up my thigh and moaned into my mouth. His cock hardened in his slacks, and he pressed it right against me.

Wow, it was big.

With one hand on my leg and the other deep in my hair, he made me feel more desirable than I ever had in my life. He was the kind of man who made me feel like a woman. He squeezed my ass with his strong hand, making me wince in pleasure against him.

He started to grind into me, rubbing his cock right along my clit.

Damn, he was gonna make me come like this.

He stuck his tongue in my mouth and circled mine, kissing me like it was his profession. He breathed into my mouth while he fisted more of my hair, taking me like I was served on a platter just for him to enjoy.

He could take me then and there, and I wouldn't stop him.

He pulled away, breaking our kiss just when it started to turn more intense.

He must have changed his mind. He must have realized what this would do to our friendship.

I hid my disappointment as best as I could.

He pressed his forehead to mine. "Let's go to my place."

He got me on the bed then peeled his shirt off. His slacks came next, along with his boxers.

"Damn..." I stared at all nine inches of his length and couldn't think of something classier to say. Actually, saying nothing would have been the classy move. He was so thick and long I could hardly believe it. Good thing I was soaked enough to get him inside.

My dress was unzipped, so he pulled it from my body then unclasped my bra with two fingers. Next, he moved for my black thong and pulled it down.

I had stretch marks, gifts from both of my girls. The bedroom lights were on, and I stiffened in embarrassment, not wanting him to see the ugly lines that now scarred my body. My figure had gone back to what it used to be, but the lines never faded away.

Ace must have understood my reaction because he said, "I wouldn't be this hard if I didn't think you were beautiful." He kneeled down and pulled me to the edge of the bed. He sealed his mouth over my opening and kissed me, giving me lots of tongue and enthusiasm.

"Oh god..." I lay back and arched my spine, loving his warm mouth on me. He circled my clit with precision, stimulating my body in new ways. I hadn't had this kind of passion in so long. The heat between Evan and me died the second that bimbo walked into his life. It was like he forgot why he'd married me to begin with.

Ace blew over my opening then kissed me again, his strong hands pinning my legs back as he devoured me.

My hand fisted his hair, and I moaned louder than I meant to, telling the entire neighborhood that I hadn't gotten laid in forever.

He sucked me hard before he rose to his feet, my arousal shining on his lips.

I was in heaven right now. I already knew Ace was sexy, but damn. He wasn't just hot, but he was a master at touching a woman. In high school, he was cute. But he was thin and quiet. In college, he started to hit the gym religiously and turned into one of the sexiest men on the planet.

And now I got to enjoy him.

He pulled out a condom from his nightstand then handed it to me. "Do the honors, baby."

I felt the foil in my fingertips but didn't rip it open. Instead, I tossed it on the bed beside me then sat up, my face right in his crotch. I grabbed him by the base and licked his head like a lollipop. My tongue felt the grooves along his head, and I swiped at the drop of arousal that formed on the surface. It tasted like a man's desire, and that revved my engine even more.

His fingers moved around the back of my neck, and he took a deep breath, his breath hissing through his teeth. He looked down at me, wearing an expression sexier than any other he'd worn before.

My fingers gripped his base as I moved my mouth all the way down. I slowly pushed him into the back of my throat, hoping I wouldn't gag from lack of experience. I hadn't given head in a very long time. Ace was bigger than Evan, so it felt like a whole new obstacle I had to overcome.

His fingers moved into my hair, and he moaned as my wet mouth took him in.

I was becoming more soaked by the minute, my wetness sliding down onto his sheets below me. There would be a spot when I moved, and I hoped he would think it was sexy. I flattened my tongue and continued to push him to the back of my throat, doing my best not to gag and enjoy him.

Ace closed his eyes and moaned, his cock hardening even more as I sucked him off.

He had just made me feel incredible, and I wanted to do the same to him. I used my hand to jerk him at the same time, stroking his cock as I sucked him off.

He pulled my head away slowly, getting his dick out of my mouth. "You're too good at that..." He grabbed the condom from the bed and rolled it on, the latex stopping near the base of his cock.

He laid me back on the bed and moved on top of me, his muscular frame causing us both to sink into the mattress. He separated my thighs with his knees and pressed his cock inside me, sliding through my wetness abruptly.

I let out a quiet cry and dug my nails into his arms, not used to the thick intrusion. I hadn't had sex in so long, and my body wasn't used to having a man inside me, especially a man like Ace.

But it felt so good.

He rocked into me immediately, sinking into me balls deep before he pulled out again. His powerful frame moved against mine easily, taking me roughly, like I thought every man should take a woman.

I already wanted to come.

Ace pressed his face close to mine and watched my reactions, staying in tune with me and understanding what I liked and what I loved. He was the kind of man who got off on pleasing a woman, not just pleasing himself.

We'd been friends for nearly fifteen years, but this didn't

feel weird. Not once did I stop and feel uncomfortable since he was my friend. All I felt was sexual desire for this man, and I wanted him to fuck me even harder than he was now.

I pulled him tighter against me, wanting all of his length every time he thrust, and kissed him hard on the mouth. My fingers dug into his tight ass, and I felt his muscles flex every time he moved.

Damn, he was hot.

In record-breaking time, he sent me into a climax. I had to stop kissing him because my body needed to scream. My high-pitched voice filled his bedroom, the echoes bouncing back at us. "God...yes." It was the most intense orgasm I'd ever had. It shattered me from head to toe and made my throat strain from the scream I just released. I couldn't remember the last time I came like that, feeling so satisfied and so sexy. Most of the time, I just felt like a mom who cleaned the kitchen table ten times a day because of the mess my girls made. But now I felt like a woman.

It felt so good I couldn't help but think I owed him something. He'd just given me an incredible gift, and I needed to return the favor. I rolled him onto his back and straddled his hips. I shoved his cock back inside me and rode him like a woman on a mission. I didn't think twice about my stretch marks. I didn't think twice about the fact that I was a mom. I let my emotions take control, and I fucked him vigorously even though I'd been out of the game for a while.

He gripped my hips and moaned through the thrusts. He held himself up on one arm and wrapped the other around my waist. Sometimes he stared at my tits, and sometimes he looked me in the eye. He looked just as sexy below me as he did on top of me. "Damn...that feels good."

I ground my clit against his muscular body, and I fucked my way into another orgasm. It was just as hot and bright, sending shivers down my spine. My body flushed with heat, and I felt sweat form on the back of my neck.

Watching me come apart must have triggered him into his own orgasm because he pulled me tight against him and released with a moan, getting every inch of his length inside me as he filled the tip of the condom. "Fuck...yeah." He thrust into me a few more times as he finished, enjoying the remainder of his high before it completely slipped away.

I rolled off him and lay beside him, my chest rising and falling as I tried to regain my breath. Every part of my body felt incredible. I'd just had the best sex, and now I actually felt satisfied. I actually felt sexy. I didn't compare myself to that bimbo Evan left me for because Ace made me feel desirable.

But now I was exhausted and didn't want to move.

Ace walked into the bathroom and cleaned himself off before he came back to me. He lay beside me on the bed, and despite how sweaty we were, he wrapped his arm around my waist and lay against me. He closed his eyes immediately, ready to go to sleep.

His bedroom was dark and cool, and I could definitely sleep well there. It would be nice to sleep with a sexy man rather than sleep alone for once. But I had two little girls at home waiting for me. They were probably asleep by now, but my sitter was waiting for me to return.

I didn't want to get up, but I forced my body to move.

Ace grabbed my wrist. "Where do you think you're going?"

"I've got to get home to my girls."

He sighed before he released my wrist, knowing I couldn't stay there.

I got out of bed and got dressed, putting on my wet panties and dress.

Ace got dressed too, putting on jeans, a t-shirt, and a hoodie. He walked me to the front door, his eyes lidded with sleepiness.

I turned around before I walked out. "That was fun... Thank you." I probably shouldn't have said that. It made it sound like he was doing me a favor, which wasn't sexy. But it'd been so long since I'd been with someone, and getting back on my feet was a little difficult.

He smiled before he kissed me on the mouth. "It was my pleasure." He walked out and shut the door behind him, intending to walk me home.

"You don't need to do that."

"It's not safe for you to walk home alone."

"Not safe?" I asked. "We're in the safest town in America."

"You could still trip and fall in the dark."

"I live right up the street."

He walked down the steps to the road. "Shut up, I'm walking you."

I rolled my eyes even though I found the gesture sweet.

He walked me a few blocks over and took me to my doorstep. The lights from the living room were on because my sitter was sitting on the couch watching TV. The lights in the bedrooms were off because the girls were fast asleep.

I looked at Ace and didn't know what to say. It didn't seem like the time or place to have a discussion about our new relationship. We were both tired, and I had to let my babysitter go home.

He took the reins. "Good night." He pulled me in for a hug before he kissed me.

Just a hug from him was incredible. He made me feel petite and safe in those big arms. "Good night."

I let my arms slip away from his waist then walked up the stone steps to the house. When I turned around, he was still standing there with that boyish smile on his face. His hands were in his pockets, and he waited for me to walk inside.

An excitement I hadn't felt in an eternity formed in my stomach. I felt my cheeks flush all over again. It was a kind of happiness I hadn't felt in so long. I hoped this was the beginning of something great, a new start.

14

BREE

Cypress walked beside me in just a t-shirt and jeans even though it was a cool evening. He didn't bring a sweater to work, but he didn't seem to mind it. Since he was a foot taller than me, he walked at a pace I had to force myself to match. "Why were you in such a hurry to get out of there?"

I hoped Amelia would make a move on Ace. She told me she'd been alone for the past year, and I knew she needed to get some action. Ace was a great guy, and he was amazing with Rose and Lily. He could be a manwhore sometimes, but he had my full approval. "Just tired."

"We didn't even finish sweeping the floor."

"Amelia will take care of it."

Cypress stared at me suspiciously, knowing I was hiding something.

"Just don't worry about it, alright?" We approached our street. The fog had settled in, so the stars weren't visible. There was something special about Carmel that prevented it from having a black sky. It was always a shade of blue, no matter what time it was. It had something to do with the coast, the reflective capability of the clouds.

"Alright. I'll mind my own business."

We arrived at his house first.

"Well, goodnight." I didn't want another intimate moment with him. When he held me the other night, something inside me had definitely softened. For a second, I didn't see him as the cheating asshole anymore.

Cypress didn't walk up the steps to his house. His eyes were trained on me, and he wasn't blinking.

That wasn't a good sign.

"Let's have a glass of wine by the fire. Dino would love to see you."

He was using the dog against me. Not fair. "I'm pretty tired…"

"I've got three king beds inside."

It was eleven thirty at night. I knew exactly what he was doing, and his invitation was nowhere near just friendly. "I'll talk to you tomorrow, Cypress." I turned away so I wouldn't have to look at that handsome face a moment longer.

Cypress watched me go without putting up any argument.

It was unlike him to be so easygoing about it, but I wasn't going to complain. I walked inside my house and finally felt safe from his intrusive gaze. He had a way of looking at me that made me feel hollow, like he could see every single emotion and thought as it drifted across my mind.

I turned on the lights then stripped my sweater off. I hung it in the closet before I walked farther into the room. All the shades were open because I never closed them during the day. I preferred natural light over artificial ones any day. Besides, it used less energy.

I glanced into his house, wondering if he was going straight to bed.

He definitely hadn't gone to bed.

He was doing pull-ups in his living room, a bar placed across the doorway that led to his backyard. He was stripped down to his boxers, his entire muscled frame visible. He still had muscular thighs and long legs. His arms bulged with power, his triceps and biceps were plump with strength. His chest was expansive and thick, and he had an eight-pack that would put any professional model to shame.

My mouth was open, and I didn't even care.

When he finished his set, he moved to the hardwood floor and started doing push-ups. With a perfectly straight back and a tight core, he pumped them out. Dino lay on the couch and watched him with a lazy expression, like he was used to seeing Cypress do this on a regular basis.

I crept closer to the window, my fingertips resting against my parted lips. I shouldn't stare, but I couldn't help it. He was the sexiest man candy I'd ever seen. His body was unbelievable when we were together, but now he was seriously ripped.

Damn.

His body started to glisten with sweat, but he didn't falter in his workout. He did at least a hundred push-ups before he finished and rose to his feet.

At this point, my nose was pretty much pressed to the window. I rubbed my forefinger across my upper lip, thinking about heated embraces we had shared in the past. No matter how mad I was at him, I couldn't deny he was the sexiest lover I'd ever had.

Cypress ran his fingers through his hair then turned to me through the window.

Shit, I'd been caught.

I tried to fumble with the string to close the shade, pretending it was just a coincidence I'd been standing there.

But then he grabbed the top of his boxers.

And I stared again, holding my breath and disregarding how perverted I looked.

He pulled his boxers down, revealing his impressive cock for me to see. It was long, thick, and pretty damn beautiful. He held my gaze without blinking, knowing he had the upper hand in the standoff.

Because I still hadn't closed my eyes.

Jesus Christ, he was something else.

I looked like a total slut staring at him through the window with my lips still parted. It took all my strength not to swipe my tongue across my lips. When it came to a man that sexy, the past was irrelevant. I just wanted to jump on him and fuck his brains out.

My good logic was gone, and I needed to get out of the situation before I did something really stupid. I grabbed the rope and quickly pulled down the shade, hiding his perfect body from view. "Oh god." I leaned against the wall next to the window and caught my breath, unsure what Cypress and I would say to one another the next time we saw each other. *Your body is unbelievable? Your dick is beautiful? Sorry I stared at you last night?*

I walked upstairs and retreated to my bedroom on the opposite side of the house. Now I had one thing on my mind, and I wasn't going to go next door to extinguish it. I had a clear enough picture in my mind that I didn't even need him in the room.

I tossed my phone on the bed as it lit up. *I know you're gonna think about me tonight. I'm gonna think about you. May as well come over so we can think about each other together.*

I almost picked up the phone and said yes. But that would be a mistake I couldn't take back. He was reeling me in with hormones, and I was embarrassed to say I took the bait. I silenced my phone and put it on my nightstand before I got into bed.

Not that I slept.

I dreaded seeing Cypress the next morning.

What would we say to each other? Would he just grin like the confident man he was and sweep it under the rug?

Of course he would.

I walked out of the house twenty minutes earlier than I usually would in an attempt to escape without Cypress knowing.

But he walked outside at the exact same time, obviously keeping an eye on my porch and waiting for me to make my move. "Morning."

I had no reason to be embarrassed, but the second I saw him, my cheeks flushed pink. I couldn't get the picture of his naked body out of my head, and it had been deeply ingrained in my mind last night when I used my fingers to touch myself the way I wished he would touch me. "Morning."

In a blue hoodie and jeans, he walked up to me with Dino right beside him. I never saw the dog on a leash, always sticking to Cypress's side like an obedient pet. As I suspected, he wore that arrogant smile—and rocked it. "Sleep well?"

Jackass. "Yes. You?"

"I slept like a rock." He put his hands in his pockets as he walked to the end of the street.

I knew exactly what those words implied, and I felt a flush of arousal when I thought about him touching himself and thinking of me. I did my best to brush it off and take the high road, keeping my head up and holding on to my last shred of dignity. "Dino doesn't need a leash?"

"Nope. He's a smart dog." He reached down and patted him on the head as he walked at the same time. "He knows he's not supposed to go in the road and to stick to the sidewalk at all times."

"Wow."

"You're the one who taught him all that."

"I am?" I didn't think I'd be such a good dog trainer.

"Yep."

I looked down at Dino, who was looking up at me with his tongue hanging out. "He's so cute..." He had one blue eye and one brown eye. Every time I looked at that beautiful face, my heart melted.

"He's a good-looking guy."

I gave his bottom a quick pat and kept walking.

"You know, if you ever wanna borrow him or take him for a walk, he's all yours."

"Yeah?"

"Yeah. He'd love that."

We reached Dolores and turned left. Some of the locals were out, walking to the coffee shop to get their morning brew. Almost everyone had a dog, so it was common to see the sidewalk filled with them.

"You bring him to work sometimes?"

"Yeah. He likes it. Better than him staying home alone all day."

Talking about Dino was a safe topic. It had nothing to do with seeing Cypress naked last night. Worked for me.

But of course, Cypress brought it up. "Why didn't you come over?"

"Because I didn't want to."

He scoffed like that was absurd.

"I didn't."

"Your mouth was open for at least two minutes."

"I was yawning."

Cypress laughed. "Yeah, okay."

"Cypress, if you think seducing me is going to work, you're wasting your time."

"Actually, I think it was my best plan. A few more times and it should work."

"I'm not sleeping with you." Under different circumstances, maybe. But not like this.

"Why not? I want you, and you want me. I've never taken you to be a prude."

"I'm not a prude."

"Besides, I'm your husband. I know all the things that you like—all of them."

I walked a little faster, trying to end this conversation. "Where are you working today?"

Cypress finally dropped the subject. "Probably Amelia's Place. That's where I usually am in the morning."

"I guess I'll be at the café. Where does Dino go?"

"In the office upstairs or outside near the benches. Lots of people will come up and pet him, so he gets attention."

We reached the entrance to Amelia's Place and walked upstairs to the private office. Ace wasn't there like he usually was, and Amelia wasn't either.

Maybe they hooked up, and they were still together. I hoped so.

Dino hopped on one of the couches and got comfortable, laying his chin down on his paws.

"I'm surprised no one is here yet." I sat at the desk I assumed to be mine and tried to find something to do. I usually spoke to the gang about what I should be doing for the afternoon, but they all seemed to be busy with other things.

"I wouldn't worry about it." Cypress hopped up on my desk and took a seat, getting close to me on purpose.

I leaned back in my chair, intentionally putting space between us. I couldn't get over what he did to me, but my body couldn't forget how much he turned me on. I might have lost my memories for the past few years, but I knew the sex in our first relationship was unbelievable. It was the kind of physical intimacy that was hard to find.

He patted the wood under his weight. "You know how many times I've fucked you on this desk?"

My skin immediately prickled as the heat rushed through my body. I stared at him without blinking, embarrassed for something I didn't even remember doing.

He held my gaze with continued confidence. "On your back. And sometimes on your hands and knees. Pretty hot."

My throat suddenly went dry, so I swallowed. "Well, those days are over…"

"No. I think they were just paused." He hopped off the desk and walked over to his, finally giving me space.

I felt like I could breathe again.

Amelia walked in the door in jeans and a t-shirt, ready to serve food downstairs. "Morning." She immediately looked at Ace's desk and couldn't hide her disappointment when he wasn't there.

So something definitely did happen.

"Morning," Cypress said. "How was your night?"

She peeled off her sweater. "Oh...it was good." She avoided eye contact as she took a seat at her desk.

Cypress didn't notice the change in her voice.

But I certainly did. "Cypress, could you get to work downstairs?"

He turned back to me and wore a wide grin. "Bossing me around, huh? Oh, I missed that." He walked out of the office, his jeans snug against his tight ass. The fabric of his shirt bunched between his shoulder blades because of his muscular frame. He was a fine specimen, beautiful.

When he was finally gone, I turned back to Amelia. "Tell me everything."

She ran from her desk to mine and pulled up a chair. "Oh my god," she whispered, even though the only one who could hear us was Dino. "I kissed him after we closed."

"And?"

"It was so good. Ace is the best kisser in the world. Wow..."

I squeezed her wrist. "That's incredible. You just walked up and kissed him? And then what?"

"He kissed me back right away then he pressed me against the back wall. That's when things got a little heated..." She smiled and blushed the same way I did when I was embarrassed. "I wrapped my leg around his waist, and he felt me up through my clothes."

"Wow." Ace was a good-looking guy, but I'd never thought of him in that way, though I could definitely picture him being good at fooling around. "Then what happened?"

"Well...we went back to his place."

My eyes practically popped out of my head. "Amelia! Did you sleep with him?"

She shrugged, a guilty look on her face. "Never kiss and tell, right?"

I gave her wrist a playful smack. "Oh my god. How was it?"

She covered her face with her hand for a second. "Bree, you don't even know... Not only does he have the full package, but he definitely knows how to use it." She dropped her hand, unable to stop grinning.

"You're making me jealous."

"Maybe it's just because I haven't been with anyone since Evan, but the sex was out of this world. I can't remember the last time I ever felt that good, ever felt like a woman, you know?"

I'd never forgive Evan for what he did to my sister. Not only did he leave her high and dry, but he abandoned his daughters. And he made Amelia, a gorgeous woman, question her attractiveness.

"I didn't feel like a mom. I felt like a sexy woman. Ace made me feel...beautiful. I was embarrassed by my stretch marks because I know they're ugly, but he didn't care at all. Said he wouldn't be so hard if he didn't find them beautiful."

"Aww..." Ace was sexy and sweet. Who knew? "I'm happy for you."

"I'm happy for me too. I couldn't spend the night because of the girls, but I wish I could have."

"He can always stay with you next time."

"True. But I don't want to confuse the girls until I

know it's serious. After losing their father, I don't want them to see another man walk away."

"Yeah…"

"So that was my night. How was yours?"

"Wait, where does that leave you guys? Are you together-together?"

"I would assume so. We didn't talk about it because there wasn't any time. I had to get home so my sitter could leave. Next time I get a chance, I'll talk to him about it."

"So…is his body as nice as it looks?"

"You have no idea," she said with a grin. "That man is ripped from head to toe. I couldn't even dig my fingers into his skin because he's so hard."

"Wow…" The description reminded me of Cypress, but I couldn't let myself even think of that.

"So, did anything happen with Cypress last night?"

Nothing as juicy as what Amelia and Ace did, but it was still pretty saucy. "Well, Cypress was working out in his boxers, and his windows were open…so I started watching him for a while."

"You nasty bitch," she teased.

I didn't correct her. "He saw me staring at him, so he took off his boxers and showed me…his junk."

"Sounds like something he would do."

"And I stared for a while longer…and then I finally got a grip and closed the shade."

"Then what happened?"

"I went to bed."

Her face fell at the disappointing ending. "That's it?"

"He texted me and said I should come over, but I ignored him."

"If you wanted to sleep with him, why didn't you?"

"In a different circumstance, I may have. Just a

hookup. But I don't want to lead him on…" I wasn't above one-night stands. I hadn't had many of them, but I wasn't against them. I didn't have a problem using Cypress for his body, not after what he did to me. But he was determined to get me back, and I didn't want to get his hopes up just to hurt him. Even if he deserved it after what happened last time, I couldn't do that to him.

"I think he would be happy just to get laid, honestly. And if you keep an open mind to it, it might be the beginning of something great."

I still wasn't sure how I felt about it. "Why did I forgive him the first time? Did he say or do something specific?"

"I think it was his determination that changed your mind. He never gave up, so you took him seriously. And Cypress is a very ambitious person. Honestly, I think you should just give up your protests and make it work. He's not gonna let you go."

I believed her. He had the endurance of an Olympic long-distance runner.

"Just something to think about."

Not only was my sister pushing me on Cypress, but Blade and Ace were as well. They'd taken his side even though I had every right to feel this way. But I suspected if I continued to live next door to Cypress, I was bound to reconsider everything.

The door opened, and Ace walked inside in slacks and a deep blue collared shirt. He was the face of Olives, and he was a great representation of the business. He brought in a lot of new customers and gave incentives for the new ones to keep coming back. "Good morning." He gave both of us a smile before he sat behind his desk.

I waited for something more to happen, for him to kiss Amelia or something. But nothing was forthcoming.

He opened his laptop and got to work, his hair perfectly styled and his body thick and muscular. He concentrated on the bookkeeping and didn't make conversation with either one of us.

I exchanged a look with Amelia.

She only shrugged in response.

15

Amelia

I didn't really have a chance to talk to Ace that day. When he finished his bookkeeping, he said goodbye then walked to Olives for the lunch rush. He smiled and acknowledged me, but he didn't address our passion last night at all.

Maybe because Bree was there? Maybe he thought I hadn't told her yet? It was possible.

I worked my morning shift downstairs then picked up the girls from school in the afternoon. When they were old enough, they would walk home from the elementary school since it was right down the road. But for now, I picked them up every day.

I gave them their afternoon snack, helped them with their homework, and then prepared dinner. I didn't get many breaks being a mom. I worked all day at the restaurant, and then I worked the second they were home.

Those were the times when I missed Evan the most.

Having a partner really made a difference. I could handle it on my own and treasured the quality time I had with Rose and Lily, but it was nice when Evan would take care of dinner so I could shower and do my hair. Now I had to juggle everything on my own. Cypress and the guys already helped more than they should, and I'd be totally lost without them.

I could never show them just how much I appreciated them.

A knock sounded at the door, and I assumed it was my sister. We'd been spending a lot of time together ever since she got her memory back. "It's open." I only locked my front door at night. It was a quiet neighborhood. The worst problems that ever happened was when squirrels went through my garbage can.

Ace walked inside, looking sexy as hell in low-slung jeans and a t-shirt. He wore that handsome smile I hadn't stopped thinking about since I'd woken up that morning. When we saw each other at the office, he acted as if we didn't hook up last night, but maybe that was because my sister was there. "I was at the post office, and I thought I'd check your PO box while I was there." He set a stack of envelopes on the counter. "But it looks like nothing but bills."

"It's always bills—and junk mail."

"I know, right?" he said with a chuckle.

"But thanks for checking for me. Saved me a trip."

"No problem." He leaned against the counter and crossed his arms over his chest. "We're going out to Cultura for some drinks. Wanna come?"

Maybe at the end of the night we could hook up again. "Yeah, sure. I'll see if Sara can watch the girls."

"Awesome. It's taco Tuesday." He walked into the living room where the girls were finishing their homework. "There's my little monsters." He kneeled down and hugged each of them before he sprinkled a kiss on their foreheads.

"You wanna color with us, Uncle Ace?" Rose asked as she handed him a pink coloring pencil.

"Yeah," Ace said. "I suppose I can spare a few minutes." He sat on the floor beside Rose and helped color her picture. They worked together silently, filling in the flowers and teapots around the sketch. Lily stopped coloring and chose to watch them instead.

Seeing Ace fit in with my girls gave me ideas I shouldn't have. Despite what happened between Evan and me, I did enjoy being married. I did enjoy being in love…while it lasted. After being alone for a year, I wanted to have that again—even if it didn't last forever.

I took the seat beside Lily on the ground and helped her with her own book.

"You're gonna color that flower brown?" Rose asked incredulously.

"Yeah," Ace said. "Why not?"

"Flowers aren't brown," Lily said. "They're pretty colors."

"Brown is a pretty color," Ace said. "It's the color of my hair."

Rose and Lily both chuckled.

Ace finished the picture with Rose before he stood up. "I'll see you later, girls."

"Bye, Uncle Ace," they both said.

I walked Ace to the front door, hoping for a soft kiss on the lips. Even a hug would have been nice. Anytime those strong arms were wrapped around me, I felt a jolt of happiness. Nothing like a strong man to make me feel like a woman.

"We're meeting at eight. Let me know if you can make it."

"Yeah, sure."

He smiled then walked out.

I thought it was weird I didn't even get a hug. Was it because the girls were in the next room? Maybe I was overthinking it. If he had a problem with last night, he wouldn't have dropped by to begin with.

I had nothing to worry about.

16

Bree

I left for the bar right after work after changing in the bathroom. I found a short, tight black dress in my closet when I went through my wardrobe the other night. It was backless, and it was so cute that it needed to be worn.

Heels over four inches were illegal in Carmel, so I wore black sandals to match my dress. I walked inside and spotted Blade and Ace at a standing table in the center of the room.

Blade whistled under his breath. "Wow, you look like a woman."

"A pretty woman," Ace said.

"I always look like a woman," I argued. "Do you normally think I'm a dude at work?"

Blade shrugged. "Dude-ish."

I smacked his arm before I walked to the bar. "I'm gonna get something."

"Don't expect to pay for it," Ace said. "Not looking like that."

I'd have to give him another smack when I came back. I stood at the bar and waited for the bartender to notice me. He was helping customers at the far left, but he finished up what he was doing and came right up to me. He was supercute. Light-colored hair and dimples in his cheeks when he smiled. He must earn a good living in tips from being a handsome man. "What can I get the pretty lady?"

And I'm sure he made a little extra from flirting with all the customers. "Something strong."

"Ooh…I like where this is going. How about an Old Fashioned?"

"Sounds perfect."

He pulled out a glass and got to work. He added the bitters then wedged a slice of orange on the glass. "This one is on the house. And the next one will cost you your phone number."

I guess he was actually coming on to me. "And the drink after that?"

He winked. "Let's find out."

He was a smooth talker. "I'm Bree."

"Hello, Bree." He shook my hand. "I'm Finn. New around here?"

"No, I've been living here for a few years." I didn't tell him about my head trauma. Not really a conversation for the first encounter. "Just didn't get out much."

"Looks like you're ready to mingle now."

I smiled but didn't blush. "I guess so."

An arm circled my waist, and the scent of pine needles teased my nose. "Hey, Finn. Looks like you just met my wife."

Goddammit, Cypress.

Finn couldn't hide his confusion. He glanced at me then turned back to Cypress. "Your wife, huh?"

"Yeah." Cypress looked down at me, pissed and affectionate at the same time. "She's a bit wild sometimes, but saddled nonetheless."

"I'm not his wife," I said quickly. "It's not like that—"

"It is like that." Cypress set a twenty on the counter. "And I'll pay for her drinks." He pulled me away from the counter and toward the table where the guys were waiting.

"Cypress." I twisted out of his grasp. "What the hell was that?"

"What the hell was what?" He held up his left hand where his wedding ring sat. "We. Are. Married."

"It's just a technicality."

"A technicality that the state of California recognizes."

"Well, we should get a divorce so the state can recognize that too."

He grabbed my arm and pulled me closer into him. "What happened to keeping an open mind?"

"I am keeping an open mind."

"No, it looks like you're flirting with the bartender."

"It's not like I'm riding his cock for my birthday." I stormed off and walked to the table, taking the place right beside Blade.

Cypress took a moment to sheathe his anger before he joined us.

Blade and Ace had both spotted our little argument and looked uncomfortable. They ate the tortilla chips on the table and drank their beers. "So, how are the Hestons doing this evening?" Ace asked.

"Don't call us that," I snapped.

"You should check your license," Blade said. "You might be surprised by what's on there."

I wanted to throw my drink in his face, but I reminded myself that Blade hadn't done anything wrong. No one had done anything wrong. This was the situation, and we just had to deal with it.

Cypress came closer to me, his arm touching mine.

I downed my drink and let the fire erupt in my belly. I knew Cypress would cockblock me every chance he had. Amelia wasn't joking about his determination. But my catty comment had silenced him immediately.

Amelia walked inside a moment later, looking like a perfect ten in her blue dress and heels. There was no way Ace would be able to stop staring at her all night. Every guy in the bar already was.

"Wow." Blade looked her up and down. "You make Bree look like a troll."

"Uh, excuse me," I said defensively. "You just said I looked pretty."

"And you do," Blade said. "But she looks even prettier."

Amelia blushed.

Even though the comment was a little rude, I let it slide. I wanted my sister to feel pretty tonight. Luck hadn't been on her side for the past few years. She deserved to have the spotlight.

"I'm gonna buy you a drink," Cypress told her. "What can I get you?"

"That's sweet," she said. "You don't have to do that."

"Yeah, I'll buy her a drink," Blade said as he pulled out his wallet.

"Nope." Ace jogged to the bar. "I got it."

"Wow, Amy," I said. "I've never had three guys fight to buy me a drink before."

"Because I'd kill them if they tried." Cypress drank his beer like his comment was appropriate.

Ace returned and set a glass of wine in front of her. "Pinot Noir."

She smiled as she took the glass. "Thank you." She sipped it, looking like a woman in heaven.

I was happy for my sister. I hadn't witnessed her devastation when Evan left, but I could see the memories deep in her eyes. Now she was out and enjoying life. Ace clearly made her happy. I could see the way she stiffened when she was around him.

Cypress stuck to me like glue. "How was work?"

"Good. How was your day?"

"Good." He didn't mention our sexual standoff to anyone. That seemed like something he would mention to the guys, but it must not have come up yet. I'm sure they would have dropped a joke by now if it had.

Whenever we weren't talking, I could feel the sexual tension. He wanted to grab me by the hair and bend me over the table then and there. I couldn't read his thoughts, but I'd bet everything I had that I was right.

Blade talked about work and our next quarterly tax payment. That seemed to be all we ever talked about whether we were working or not. Ace mentioned a crazy guy at the restaurant who said he ordered fish and got chicken instead, but it ended up being fish.

Every time Cypress adjusted himself, he moved closer to me. I wasn't sure if he was doing it on purpose, but I suspected he was.

I was either thirsty or nervous because I finished my entire drink in record time. Five minutes and it was gone. "I'll be back."

Cypress snatched my glass and walked away, heading to the bar for me.

I rolled my eyes and turned back to everyone else.

"I wouldn't fight it," Blade said as he looked at the TV. "It's gonna happen anyway. May as well just go with it."

"I should just settle for a cheater?" I asked incredulously. "Would you settle for a cheater?"

Blade responded by drinking from his glass.

When I turned to glance at Cypress, a pretty blonde was talking to him at the bar. In a short-ass dress that could barely contain her tits, she was putting the moves on him. I didn't need to hear what she was saying to know that's what was going on. I turned back to the gang.

Blade grinned. "Jealous?"

"No." The answer flew out of my mouth quicker than I wanted it to. "I was just wondering where my drink was."

"You're so jealous," Ace said. "It's written all over your face."

"I'm not jealous," I repeated. "Seeing him with another woman just brings back old memories." Even if I wanted to make it work with Cypress, I doubted I could trust him again. When I saw him at the bar, I immediately pictured Vanessa riding him on his bed. I'd lost most of my memories, but I wish that was the one that had disappeared instead.

"Ouch," Ace said. "It's gonna take him a while to live that down."

"He'll never live it down," I whispered.

Cypress returned with my refill and set it on the table. "There you go, sweetheart."

"Had fun with your little friend?" I stirred my glass without looking at him.

He smiled. "She's a regular at Amelia's Place."

"I bet she is," I mumbled.

His arm circled my waist, sending electricity down my spine. "Don't worry, she knows I'm married."

"Well, you aren't married," I pointed out.

"Our marriage license doesn't agree with that statement," he replied.

Blade sighed and rubbed the back of his neck. "You guys are so cute."

Amelia chuckled into her glass.

I wanted to kick Cypress under the table. "We're getting a divorce. That's final."

"I'd like to see you try," Cypress threatened.

"When I get married, I hope I'm as happy as you guys," Ace said sarcastically.

Cypress continued on, "You wanted to sleep with me last night. You get jealous when you see me with another woman. And you're gonna keep saying we aren't married?"

"Whoa, you almost slept together?" Blade asked.

"No," I said immediately. "That's not what happened."

"I was working out in my living room in my boxers, and she stared at me through the window." Cypress threw me under the bus.

"Wow, someone's a pervert," Ace said. "If I did that to someone, I'd go to jail."

"It wasn't like that," I said defensively.

"She didn't close her mouth for several minutes. And I swear, she licked her lips," Cypress said.

"I did not," I snapped. "I almost did, but I didn't."

Blade raised an eyebrow. "So you were standing there looking at him with your mouth open?"

Cypress grinned then took a drink.

I'd incriminated myself by accident, and now I really did look like a pervert. "I shut the shade and went to bed."

"You did not go to sleep," Cypress said. "I know that for a fact."

Ace and Blade laughed.

Amelia even chuckled.

He was right. I didn't go to sleep. But I didn't want to talk about masturbating to the thought of my naked ex-boyfriend or husband. Whatever. "It's not like you don't stare at me."

"You bet your ass I stare at you," Cypress said. "I check out your tits and ass every single day. Husband privileges."

Now I wanted to throw my drink in his face. "Let's talk about something else."

"Like what?" Blade asked. "The only interesting thing going on in our lives is the two of you and work."

"Have you met anyone?" I asked, even though I knew he would have already told me if he had.

"Not yet," Blade said. "But when the time is right, she'll appear. And I know she's gonna be smokin'."

"Not all of us can have a perfect ten for a wife." Cypress moved his arm around my waist.

I slapped his hand away. "If I were a perfect ten, you wouldn't have fucked Vanessa."

He dropped his hand and sighed.

Ace set down his drink. "Ouch. Bree, don't you think you're being a little harsh?"

"Just a little?" Blade pressed.

"No, I really don't." I drank from my glass and avoided their gaze.

Cypress looked at them and shook his head, giving some kind of signal.

Blade watched the TV before he noticed someone across the room. "Ace, your lady is here."

His lady?

Amelia's eyes narrowed, and she slowly set her glass on the table.

Ace looked to the door and watched Lady walk toward him in a miniskirt and a slutty top. She wore a jean jacket to keep her warm, but there was no way she was staying warm in those rags. "Hey, baby." He wrapped his arm around her waist and gave her a kiss. "What are you drinking?"

What the hell was going on?

"I'll have whatever you're having," she whispered.

"Coming right up." He tapped her on the ass and walked to the bar.

I looked at Amelia, who was pale in the face. I thought something else had happened between her and Ace, but judging from the shock on her face, the conversation never took place.

Ace didn't behave any differently. He fetched Lady the drink and returned, his arm moving around her waist. "How was work?"

"Boring," she said. "I was excited when you texted me."

I still couldn't figure out what was going on. Did Ace sleep with Amelia and then forget it happened? Did he hit his head as hard as I hit mine?

Blade talked to Lady like everything was normal. Cypress watched the TV in the corner, keeping his eyes on the score.

I made eye contact with Amelia.

She looked like she was about to cry. She pulled her phone out of her purse and read a text message that was never sent. "Sara is sick and needs me to come home. I'll catch up with you guys later." She didn't say goodbye to anyone and nearly tripped on her way out the door.

Everyone stared at her, knowing something was off because she'd left so abruptly.

Lady was the first one to say something. "Is she okay?"

"She's got two little girls at home." I covered for my sister, not wanting her to be humiliated. I wanted to chase after her and comfort her, but if I did, everyone would know something was wrong.

An hour later, Lady excused herself to the bathroom.

That's when I pounced. "Ace, what the hell?"

He was about to take a drink when he stilled. "What? You want another drink?"

"No," I snapped. "You slept with Amelia last night, and you're still seeing Lady? What the hell, asshole?"

Blade's head snapped in Ace's direction so fast he nearly broke his neck.

Cypress's hand tightened on his glass, and he ground his teeth together so hard I could practically hear it.

"You slept with Amelia?" Blade asked. "Why didn't you tell me?"

"I know exactly why he didn't tell me," Cypress said coldly.

"You think you can do that to my sister and get away with it?" I demanded. "The second we get outside, I'm kicking your ass."

"Whoa, hold on." Ace raised both hands. "I didn't know she told anyone about that…"

"What does it matter?" I pointed at my chest. "I'm her sister. Of course she told me."

"And I'll help my wife kick your ass," Cypress said.

It was the only time I didn't give him shit for calling me his wife.

"Everyone, chill." Ace lowered his hands. "I didn't think last night meant anything. I thought that was just two friends hooking up."

"When does Amelia just hook up with someone?" I exclaimed. "That's not her, and you know it."

Ace ran his hand through his hair, clearly uneasy about the whole thing. "I know she's been single for a long time, and I thought she just wanted to get laid. She just walked up to me at the restaurant and kissed me. She didn't tell me she had feelings for me or anything. And when a hot woman kisses me like that, I ain't gonna say no."

"So you're okay with cheating on Lady?"

"I didn't cheat. She and I aren't exclusive."

"So if I told Lady about Amelia, she would be just fine with that?" I asked.

"I'm sure it would make her uncomfortable, but she wouldn't be mad," Ace said. "And I'd really appreciate it if you didn't tell her that."

"We'll see," I threatened.

"Dude, I can't believe you hooked up with Amelia," Blade said. "That's just insane."

"Actually, he asked for a death sentence," Cypress said.

"Is that why she left?" Ace asked. "Because Lady made her uncomfortable?"

"She left because she thought you guys were a thing," I explained. "Not just two friends hooking up."

When Ace realized the truth, he actually looked sad.

He lowered his gaze then ran his hand through his hair again. "Honestly, I didn't know. She and I hardly said two words to each other. We hooked up, and I walked her home. That was it. I stopped by the house earlier to bring her the mail, and everything was normal. I just assumed nothing had changed."

My anger dimmed—slightly.

Cypress looked just as pissed as he had from the beginning.

"Dude, you shouldn't hook up with friends," Blade said. "Never goes well."

"It all happened so fast," Ace said. "She kissed me, and before I knew it, we were grinding against the wall and her dress was up."

"It's called self-control," Cypress said.

"You're one to talk," I jabbed.

Cypress sighed then took a drink.

"And she's a damn good kisser," Ace continued. "Like, wow. Maybe it's because she hasn't been with a guy in so long, but she's charged."

"What are you going to do?" Blade asked.

"I—" Ace stopped talking when Lady appeared at his side. "I love fried cheese sticks. Wish they had some here."

Worst cover-up ever.

"Yeah, me too," Blade said as he joined in. "Can't get enough fried cheese…"

Lady didn't find the conversation suspicious at all. "I'm a jalapeno popper kind of girl."

Ace didn't put his arm around her again. He rested both of his elbows on the table, his eyes heavy with thought.

Lady popped a few chips into her mouth before she picked up on Ace's mood. "Everything alright?"

"Yeah." He straightened and shoved some chips into his mouth. "I was just thinking about work. You know, work never sleeps." He drummed his fingers on the table, getting lost in his thoughts again.

Lady hooked her arm through his, being affectionate even though Ace didn't want to be.

Blade cleared his throat then changed the subject. "Too bad the highway is closed down before Big Sur. Thought we could go hiking one day—"

"I've got to go." Ace pulled away from Lady. "I just realized I have something to do at the office."

"Uh...okay." Lady dropped her hand and gripped the edge of the table.

"You want me to give you a lift back to Monterey?" Ace asked.

"No, I drove," Lady said. "Are you sure you're alright?"

"Yeah, I'm fine," he said quickly. "Well, I'll walk you to your car." He didn't say goodnight to any of us before he took her hand and pulled her out of the restaurant.

"What was that about?" Blade asked.

"He's probably going to talk to Amelia," I said.

"He better be." Cypress was in the same sour mood he'd been in since he found out what Ace did. "But I'm gonna give him a black eye anyway."

Cypress was quiet on the way home. He didn't make small talk with me. In fact, he didn't say anything at all. With his hands in his pockets, he walked straight without turning to look at me.

I kept my eyes on the road, just as disappointed by the way the events had unfolded. "I'm not sure how I feel about Ace right now. People hook up. I can't really be mad at him for it."

"There's nothing wrong with hooking up with someone." He spoke quietly, his masculine voice barely above a whisper. "Screw whoever you want. Have fun. Whatever. Don't fuck your friend who's been going through a rough year. Unacceptable."

"He seemed genuine, that he didn't know how she felt. And she did walk up to him and kiss him... It wasn't like she asked him out on a date."

"No excuse."

I probably shouldn't say what I was going to say, but I said anyway. "You're being awfully harsh when you've done something a lot worse."

"And you won't hear me make an excuse for it. It took years for everyone to forgive me. I paid my dues and accepted my punishment. That's why I'm here now."

"What punishment?"

"Losing you for a year. And then losing you again for another year. It's like that accident happened just to torture me, to force me to live on while the love of my life didn't remember anything good about me. It sucked."

I swallowed the lump in my throat, feeling sadness when I shouldn't. "Where did we go on our honeymoon?"

"Maui."

"Where did we get married?"

"The Perry House in Monterey."

"When's our wedding anniversary?"

"Halloween."

I turned to him in surprise when we reached 7th. "We got married on Halloween?"

"Yeah."

"Why?" I loved Halloween as much as the next person, but it wasn't significant to either of us.

"We officially got back together on Halloween. You'd told me you could never forgive me for what I'd done, so I finally let you go. But later that night, something changed your mind. You came to my house, kissed me, and that was it."

I took my time walking down the hill in my sandals. They weren't very tall, but they were tall enough that I needed to be careful. I tried to picture this memory, but my mind kept turning blank. "Was our wedding Halloween themed?"

"We gave out masks as a party favor, and we had some scary stuff for the photo booth. But that was it."

"Oh..."

We reached Casanova then turned right. When we reached Cypress's house, a quiet bark came from the door.

"Dino must want to get out," Cypress said. "He'd been cooped up all evening."

"Poor guy."

Instead of hugging me or trying to convince me to come inside, he turned to the steps. "Good night."

I was finally getting a night off. I didn't have to reject his advances and stop him from kissing me. "Cypress?"

"Hmm?" He turned around, his powerful arms resting by his sides.

"You're really upset?" I was asking a question, but I wasn't entirely sure what I was asking. I knew he was protective of my sister, but it surprised me how close they'd gotten while I'd been incapacitated. I distinctly remembered her wishing he was dead.

"Amelia is probably my closest friend in the world. We both had to go through a lot when Evan left and you lost your memory. She was the person I talked to when you were having a particularly bad day. She was the person I talked to when I felt like giving up. I was the person she came to when things became too difficult and she needed help. She's not my sister-in-law. She's my sister."

I bowed my head, touched by what he said. He could have just left me and moved on with his life, abandoning me and my sister. But he stayed and looked after both of us. He didn't know I was ever going to get better, so everything he did came from the heart. "I'm sorry for being so harsh on you…"

"It's okay," he whispered. "I understand."

"I don't know why I can't let it go and focus on what's happened. It's just hard for me."

"I understand that, sweetheart. You don't remember everything. I get it. What I did was really horrible. You can take all the time you need to get through it. I'm not going anywhere. I'll always be here—right next door."

I crossed my arms over my chest, fighting the cold. "How long did it take me to get over it the first time?"

He sighed as he thought to himself. "Probably six months. And even after that, you didn't really trust me. Took at least a year."

That was a long time.

"You can take even longer this time if you need it. I just want to work it out together."

"A friendship is all I can give you for now."

"That's fine," he said. "I'll take it."

"But I want a divorce."

He shook his head. "Nonnegotiable."

"I never said it was negotiable. That's what I want. What if time goes on, and I can't get over what you did? We're just gonna have to get a divorce then."

"And we'll worry about that when the time comes. But for now, we're focused on making this work."

"It makes me feel trapped. Like I don't have a choice."

He played with his wedding band on his left hand. "You're the love of my life, sweetheart. I can't let you go. I'm willing to be patient. I'm willing to be understanding. I'm willing to do whatever you want to make this work. But I'm not willing to compromise on that."

He was so stubborn. "Cypress, it's not a choice for you. I can get a divorce even if you don't want one."

"Then out of recognition for what I've done for you, could you please not do it? I've taken care of you every single day for the past eighteen months. I took care of your sister when she couldn't get out of bed. I've taken care of your business and paid all your bills. I've gone above and beyond for you. Can't you just give this to me?"

When he put it like that, I couldn't deny him. I couldn't take away something that meant the world to him. "You're basically guilting me into staying married to you."

"I'm asking you to give me time."

"How much?"

"A year."

"A year?" I asked incredulously. "Six months at the most."

"Eight."

"Six," I repeated.

"Seven."

I sighed, knowing I should do this because he'd done so much for me. I didn't see him the way he saw me, but I appreciated how devoted he was. I couldn't sweep that under the rug. "Fine. Seven months."

"Thank you." He turned around and walked up the stairs.

I walked over to my house, unable to believe I agreed to stay married to him for seven months. That meant I couldn't date anyone. That meant I really had to keep an open mind about this. I had to hope I would fall in love with my cheating ex.

Again.

17

Amelia

Was I the dumbest person in the world? Was it stupid to think Ace actually wanted to be with me? Of course, I was just a piece of ass to him. Why did I think it would lead to something more meaningful when we barely said two words to each other?

I hoped Bree wouldn't say anything to Ace or the guys. I didn't want him to be uncomfortable around me or feel bad for me. Pity would be even worse. Instead of going home, I went to the office above Amelia's Place. I couldn't put on a straight face for my girls and watch cartoons with them. They liked it when I read to them at night, and I wasn't in the mood to do that either.

I flipped on the lights and sat at my desk. We had a TV in there, but none of us ever watched it. I wasn't even sure if we had cable. Since I wasn't doing anything productive, just sitting there, I opened my laptop and did some work. At least Cypress wouldn't have to worry about it in the morning.

The knob turned on the door behind me, and I nearly

jumped out of my chair. I was used to the silence and solitude, and no one should be coming into this office unless they planned to rob it. I snatched the lamp off my desk and yanked the cord out of the outlet, ready to kick some ass.

"Whoa, it's me." Ace held up both hands like I had pointed a gun at him. "Put the lamp down."

"God, you scared the shit out of me." I set the lamp down, but I didn't plug it back in. My hand moved over my heart, and I sat back down in the wheeled desk chair. "What are you doing here?"

"Well…" He slid his hands into his pockets and walked to Cypress's desk, which was directly next to mine. "I went to your house, but Sara said you hadn't come back yet."

Oh, shit. Bree had told him. "Oh…"

"And this is the only other place you would go."

Damn, we'd known each other too long. I lowered my gaze to the floor because I was humiliated. I could only assume Bree told him everything, and I looked like a clingy girl who got her heart broken. "What did Bree tell you?" I wasn't putting my cards on the table until he put his down first.

"She told me it wasn't just a one-night stand to you. That you were under the impression that we were together…or exclusive."

I hated my sister.

"I'm so sorry, Amy. I didn't have a clue that's how you felt. I thought we just hooked up…"

"Ace, you don't need to apologize." I didn't want to lose his friendship or make our working relationship weird. "It was my fault. I was stupid, and I wasn't thinking. I don't blame you for getting the wrong impression. I wasn't very clear."

"Wow...you're gonna let me off the hook for this?"

"Well, I just don't think it's all your fault."

He crossed his arms over his chest as he looked at me. "You know I would never do anything to hurt you. You're family to me."

"I know..." He was one of the sweetest guys I'd ever met.

"I know you haven't been with anyone since Evan, and it's been...a really long time. I just thought you wanted to get laid. And I thought you came to me because you wanted it to be with someone you felt comfortable with and you wouldn't have to explain yourself. Obviously, I totally misread the situation. I should have clarified."

"It's my fault too. When I saw you with Lady...I just lost my shit."

"She and I aren't exclusive," he said. "I don't want you to think I'm a cheater or something."

"No, I know. I just...never mind." We had already established we were in different places. There was no need to explain what I thought.

"What?" he pressed.

"Nothing," I said. "I'd really like it if we could go back to being friends and forget this whole thing happened."

"We were always friends," he said gently. "We wouldn't be going back to anything. But there's something we have to talk about. I'd rather get it out in the open instead of having another misunderstanding later down the road."

"Okay..."

"Bree made it sound like you wanted something more serious with me. Is that true?"

I was backed into a corner where I didn't want to be. I wanted to lie my way out of it, but that wouldn't do me any good. If I didn't want something serious, I wouldn't have been upset about Lady in the first place. It was a moot point. "I don't know if I'd say something serious…but I think you're a great guy. I guess I've had feelings for you lately."

Ace stared at me with a stoic expression. Normally, he was easy to read, but now it was impossible to figure out his thoughts. He had a stern jaw but soft eyes. He could be ruthless but so gentle at the exact same time. He was the kind of man who used his strength to protect people, not exploit them. He was honest, loyal, and not to mention, he was great with my kids.

"It started a few months ago. I told Bree about it, and she said I should try to make a move. She said you used to have feelings for me when we were in high school, so I thought I had a chance."

"Bree told you that?"

"Well, Cypress and Blade did."

"So they knew the whole time?" he asked in surprise.

"Yeah…I made them promise not to tell you."

He rubbed the back of his neck and released a quiet sigh. "Honestly, I had no idea you felt this way. If I'd known…"

That was a rejection—plain and simple. "We're both adults here. We can move on from this."

"I did have a crush on you in high school. Well, it was more than a crush. When you started seeing Evan, I was pretty sad about it. Then when you married him, I moved on and said goodbye to that possibility. Since then, I haven't really seen you like that. I started to see you as just a friend."

I nodded, taking the rejection in stride. "I understand, Ace. You don't need to say any more."

"I'm not gonna lie. That kiss…was pretty damn good.

The sex was even better. It's something I won't forget about. It's something I'll probably jerk off to."

Heat flushed up my neck and made me feel warm everywhere. The idea of him beating himself off got me so hot and bothered. I swallowed the lump in my throat and pretended to be unaffected by it.

"But I'm not looking for anything serious right now. And I love Rose and Lily, but I'm just not in the place to be a stepfather—"

"Ace, I've never asked you to be. You're making a lot of assumptions about stuff way into the future. That's not at all what I'm thinking right now. I just know I like you, and I wanted to be with you. That's it."

"Okay. I just wanted to be straight with you so there would be no confusion between us."

I smiled. "No confusion." But I was dead inside. I should have been with Ace when I had the chance, but I'd picked a jerk instead. I was a single mom with two kids, and that's exactly how he saw me. "I'm glad we could work this out."

"Yeah, me too. And again, I'm sorry. You mean a lot to me. I would hate to lose you over something I didn't mean to do."

"You could never lose me, Ace." I rose to my feet and walked up to him. I kept space between us, doing my best not to touch him. Normally, when I was down like this, I would turn to him for comfort. I would tell him everything that happened and I was struggling with how much it hurt to get turned down. But I couldn't do that with him on this occasion.

He finally smiled. "Good. Because I'd be pretty devastated if you walked away." His hands circled my waist, and he held me against his strong chest. He felt incredible, warm and masculine. My arms automatically hugged him back, and I didn't want to pull away. I felt the chemical attraction, the undeniable pull. Did he have great sex like that all the time? I wasn't so lucky.

I cleared my throat and pulled back, having gotten too comfortable in the embrace.

When he looked down at me, his expression was different from just a second ago. That handsome smile was gone, replaced by the masculine intensity I remembered seeing when he was on top of me. He glanced at my lips but then quickly looked away, pretending he hadn't stared at them to begin with. His hands slowly slid down my arms, and he released a quiet breath as he stepped back. "Can I walk you home?"

"Yeah, sure." I didn't need to be walked home, but I was so weak that I just agreed. Anytime we touched, I felt the electrical energy travel through me quicker than lightning struck the ground.

We left the office together and walked to my house a few streets over. We didn't say anything because everything important had already been said. It would be awkward for the next few interactions we had, but after that, it would go back to normal. The gang would want to talk about it too, but the news would blow over.

We arrived at my house, and he walked me to the door. "Good night."

"Good night." I was just going to walk inside, but he hugged me instead. He pulled me into his chest again and squeezed me tightly.

Two hugs in a row. Must be my lucky day.

"Call me if you need anything."

"Okay."

His arms slid from around my body, and he stepped back. "I'll see you tomorrow."

"Alright. See you tomorrow." I watched him walk away, his shoulders looking powerful in his t-shirt. I could stare at the way his muscles shifted all day, but I knew I shouldn't look at him that way anymore.

I needed to get over him and move on.

Cypress walked into the office with two cups of coffee. "Morning." He set one on my desk before he took a seat.

"Thanks. Where's Bree?"

"The café." He sat back in the chair and put his feet on the desk. "So, you want to talk about last night?"

"I don't know. Not much to say."

"Ace said he was going to talk to you." He couldn't speak without sounding angry. His pretty eyes weren't so kind anymore. Now they were just aggressive. "Did he?"

"Yeah. We talked, and he walked me home."

"And what did he say?"

"He apologized even though it wasn't really his fault—"

"Yes, it was his fault."

"Not really. I didn't give him a good impression. I just kissed him without any explanation of what I was thinking. He's a man. Of course, he thought it was a hookup."

"You're his friend and business partner. He should have thought it through."

Cypress was more upset about it than I was, but that didn't surprise me. Once Evan and Bree were gone, he'd stepped in and became a father figure to the girls, a partner I could rely on, and an uncle all at the same time. "Give him a break, Cypress."

"I'm too mad to cut him any slack right now."

I'm sure Cypress would get over it—in time.

"What happened?"

"I told him I wanted something more serious, and he said he wasn't looking for that. So we're just going to be friends."

"I'm sorry, Amelia." He looked remorseful even though it wasn't his fault.

"I know. But that was the reaction I was expecting. Most people our age aren't looking to have kids in the mix."

"That's not true. You'll find a guy who loves your kids as much as you do. Don't worry about it. Ace is just young, you know. He's looking to fuck and drink, and that's about it."

"I know. And that's fine. I don't judge him for it."

"I don't either. But I judge him for taking advantage of you."

"He wasn't taking advantage of me," I corrected. "I put the moves on him, remember?"

"That idiot isn't an idiot. He knew what he was doing."

I smiled because that didn't add up.

"You know what I mean." He drank from his cup then licked his lips.

"Life goes on, and I'll be fine. It's not like I was in love with him."

Cypress took another sip. "You weren't?"

"No. But the idea of us being together made me happy. You know, having what you and Bree have."

He scoffed. "In case you haven't noticed, we don't have much right now."

"You'll get there, Cypress. You got her back once before. You can do it again."

"I don't know. She seems more stubborn this time, if you can believe it."

"Oh, I can," I said with a laugh. "I've known that brat for a long time. But if you put on the charm and prove you're different, she'll come around. She's not one to hold a grudge."

"She's definitely holding a grudge right now."

"But it's different, and you know it. Think about it. In her mind, the cheating just took place. Of course, she's angry. Of course, she doesn't feel anything for you. You're gonna have to convince her to fall in love with you again. It's not gonna be easy, but you already knew that. But if you don't give up, you should get there."

"I asked her not to divorce me for seven months. She agreed."

"See? Progress."

"But she wasn't happy about it. The only reason why she's giving me any kind of opportunity is because I took care of her and you for the past few years. She feels like she owes me something."

"Or maybe she just thinks it's sweet. She's not a robot. She does have feelings."

His eyes shifted to the window, and he rubbed his fingers across his chin. "I know she does."

"I say you have a good chance, Cypress. Don't give up."

"I just wish we could do it differently."

"How?"

"Like, have us living together again. Sleeping together again. Have her learn about our marriage. And then when she gets used to it, we'll be back to normal."

"Cypress, that would never work." I thought he was an

extremely intelligent man, but that idea was just dumb. "She's not in love with you. That's the problem. You've got to change that. Once you do, I'm sure she would do all of that."

"Yeah, I suppose."

"You could always try marriage counseling. Couples do that." When I found out Evan was leaving me, I'd suggested it. I was desperate to keep my marriage together for my girls…and because I still loved him.

"Yeah…I guess I could suggest it. Not sure if she would go for it, but it doesn't hurt to ask."

"Nope."

"Or…" He turned back to me. "Her older sister that she looks up to could just tell her to be with me." He grinned.

"I'll help you in any way that I can, but I'm not doing that."

"Come on, why not?"

"I'm not going to pressure her to do anything. She needs to decide on her own."

"You wouldn't be pressuring her, just guiding her."

"I still don't want to influence her. This is her life, not mine. I already tell her all the amazing things about you because they're all true. But I'm not gonna tell her that she needs to be with you and it would be a mistake to let you go. She's gotta figure that out on her own."

He drank his coffee again, his eyes heavy with sadness. We sat in mutual silence, him drinking his coffee and me working on a few things before the diner opened. Ace walked inside a moment later in jeans and a sweater.

Even in a sweater, he looked hot.

"What's up?" He walked to his desk.

"Hey," I said, being as normal as possible.

Cypress stared him down coldly and sipped his coffee.

The tension rose.

Ace took a seat and ignored Cypress's palpable hostility.

I tried to smooth things over. "Are you working tonight?"

"Yeah," Ace answered.

"You need to take a day off sometime."

"I know," Ace said with a chuckle. "I do enjoy it, though. Keeps the workers on top of their game as well."

"Well, Bree and I could always rotate in if you need a break."

"Thanks," Ace said. "I'll keep that in mind."

Cypress wouldn't stop staring at Ace, continuing to sip his coffee with imminent threat in his eyes.

Ace finally looked at him straight on. "Yes?"

"Don't come in here acting all normal and shit," Cypress snapped. "You're a fucking asshole, and you know it."

Whoa, that got ugly quick. "Cypress—"

Ace cut me off. "Amelia and I are fine, if you didn't notice. We're both adults, and we've been mature about it. We're still friends like we were before. So you need to calm down."

"I don't need to calm down," Cypress said. "She's family to me, and you know that."

"She's family to me too," Ace snapped. "You know I would never hurt her on purpose."

"But you still hurt her, dickhead." Cypress slammed his coffee down. "You were only thinking with your dick and not the rest of your brain. If you think I'm gonna let this go, you're an idiot."

"Cypress." I stared at him until he met my look. "I appreciate you being protective, but it's really okay. Ace and I are fine. We've already moved on from it. You're the only one who hasn't let it go."

Cypress grabbed his coffee again and looked out the window, dismissing the conversation.

Ace stood up again. "I'm gonna go help Bree with the café. I should be welcome there."

"Don't count on it," Cypress said under his breath.

Ace walked out.

"Cypress," I said with a sigh. "You're making it into a bigger deal than it needs to be."

"You've had feelings for him for six months," he countered. "It's not like you just thought he was cute. You have an emotional attraction to this guy. No, it's not okay."

"Well, he doesn't know that. I really downplayed how I felt about him so he wouldn't be uncomfortable. You can't get mad at him for something he wasn't aware of. I'm already embarrassed as it is, and you bringing it up is just making it worse. So please stop."

Cypress finally dropped his anger when my words sank in. "I apologize."

"It's okay. I know you meant well."

"I can't tolerate it when someone hurts someone I love."

How could I be annoyed with him when he said things like that? "I know…"

18

BLADE

I needed to bury the hatchet between my two friends before something worse erupted. It would grow until it became uncontrollable, and then it would bite all of us in the ass. When Cypress first came to our group, we gave him hell every single day. I was surprised he lasted so long.

Ace arrived at Cultura first, grabbed a beer, and then joined me at the table. "What's up?" He rested both arms on the table then looked at the TV in the corner. The Giants weren't doing so well this year, to everyone's dismay.

"I just ordered fried calamari."

"Awesome. But I was craving cheese sticks."

I guess he never realized that was just a decoy at the time. "So, how are things with Amelia?"

"Did you invite me down here just to talk about it?"

"No..."

Ace gave me a glare.

"Okay...yes."

"I'm not gonna talk about it. I'm a gentleman, alright?"

"You told me you fucked Lady in the parking lot of a Taco Bell the other day."

"Not the same thing."

"And then she sucked you off in the parking lot of a Wendy's. By the way, what's with all the fast-food places? Turn you on or something?"

"We usually get food in the middle of the night when I sleep over, and she lives down the street from those places. But by the time we get there...she's ready. Maybe she's turned on by burritos and hamburgers, but I'm certainly not."

Still weird.

"And that's not the same thing."

"It's not the same thing if she's not a woman. But I'm pretty sure she is."

"But Lady and I aren't together." The waiter brought the calamari, and Ace immediately popped a few pieces into his mouth.

"Were you and Amelia together?" I raised an eyebrow.

"No, but that's different. I respect her, alright? I'm not gonna tell you what went down. I'm not gonna tell you what her tits looked like."

"Wasn't asking." Amelia was pretty. Anyone with eyes would agree with me. But I didn't see her like that.

"Then all you need to know is we hooked up. End of story."

"And how are you now?"

"She and I are fine. We went back to being friends right away. She was super understanding about it."

"When she stormed out of here, it looked like she was about to cry...so it makes me think she's not as understanding as you think. Maybe she's just trying to cover it up because she's embarrassed."

Ace held a piece of calamari between his fingertips briefly before he put it in his mouth. "She did say she wanted more, so she was upset when she saw me with Lady. But I told her that wasn't going to happen."

"Why not? You used to be head over heels for her."

"Like ten years ago."

"Whatever. Now you have your shot."

He shook his head. "I don't know... I don't think it would work out."

"Because you don't feel that way about her?"

"I just don't see myself being a husband or father, honestly. And that's exactly what she's looking for. I don't have it in me."

"What are you talking about?" He was the most responsible guy I knew. "You're fine, Ace."

"I like bouncing from woman to woman. I like not having responsibilities. I like how uncomplicated my life is. If I get together with Amelia, everything will change. I'll have to be a stepfather."

"But you love those kids."

"Of course, I do. But I can't handle the responsibility."

There was something he wasn't telling me, but I couldn't figure out what it was. Some of his reasons made sense, but at the same time, they didn't. When we were freshmen in high school, his dad packed his stuff and took off. Ace never saw him again. Maybe that was the reason. "I feel like you aren't telling me something."

He looked at the TV. "I'm not. Just being honest."

Cypress walked inside and stilled when he saw Ace sitting at the table.

I pulled out the chair. "Don't be a drama queen and sit down."

Cypress hesitated before he sank into the chair.

Ace stared at him with a stoic expression, obviously unsure what to expect.

"I tricked you both into coming down here so we could get through this," I said. "We're all best bros, and we can't have anything weird between us."

"We aren't best bros," Cypress said. "Stop calling us that."

"Whatever," I said. "You two need to work this out."

"We aren't women," Cypress said. "We're over it."

"I distinctly remember you calling me a dickhead this morning," Ace said before he popped another piece in his mouth.

"Well, you were," Cypress snapped. "But Amelia told me she wanted me to drop it so...I'll drop it."

"Good," Ace said. "It's not like I did something terrible like cheat on her."

It was a low blow, and we all knew it.

Cypress didn't argue or get upset. All he did was sigh. "I'm sorry for overreacting. Are we cool?"

Ace considered the apology before he nodded. "We're cool." He fist-bumped him. "Sorry about the cheater comment."

"It's okay," Cypress said. "I've gotten used to it."

19

BREE

A knock sounded on my door, and I knew it could only be one person. I'd just finished dinner, and now I sat in the living room with the TV on. The hardwood floors of my house made everything echo, so his knock sounded a million times louder than it should.

I was in my sweatpants and a t-shirt, but thankfully, my hair was done and I still had my makeup on. I opened the door and greeted him as friendly as possible. "Hey."

He was holding a box of firewood. "Hey. Just restocked my logs and thought you could use some." Even though it looked heavy, he held it like it didn't weigh anything at all.

"Oh, that was nice of you."

He continued to stand there in a tight t-shirt that looked great on his shoulders and chest. "Can I come in, then?"

"Oh, sorry." I'd been too preoccupied with his appearance that I couldn't think straight. I stepped out of the way so he could walk inside.

He carried it to the fireplace then stacked the logs on

the log holder. Each piece resonated against the iron, emitting a low sound as the pile grew higher and higher. Cypress kneeled on the floor, and his muscles shifted under his t-shirt as he moved.

He was far too handsome for me not to notice. I remembered the first day I laid eyes on him, my tongue practically fell out of my mouth. When he stood up, I stared at his tight ass and wished I could dig my fingers into that big piece of muscle.

He turned around and dusted his hands on his jeans. "Need anything else?"

"No. Thanks for bringing that. I've been out for a while but haven't thought about getting more."

"No problem." He walked past me, his thick arm brushing against mine.

I still got chills when he touched me. I knew it was just physical attraction, but it was a powerful sensation. I turned away, feeling my throat go dry.

"Have a good night."

"Yeah…" I watched him walk out and take the stone steps down. I wanted to say something, but nothing came to mind. I wasn't even sure what I wanted. Living alone in this big house with my loneliness echoing back at me could be exhausting. I wanted to go out and mingle with people, but I promised him I'd wait seven months before I got a divorce.

He walked back over to his house and shut the door.

I got a fire going and listened to it crackle as the TV played. The light from the flames licked up the walls and gave my living room a nice glow. I couldn't help but wonder what Cypress was doing. Was he watching TV like I was? Was he working out shirtless?

My curiosity got the best of me, so I stood up and

walked past my windows toward the kitchen, glancing into his house.

I got lucky, because he stepped into the living room with just a towel around his waist. His hair was wet because he must have just gotten out of the shower. He stood behind his couch and looked at the TV, probably wanting to see the score of the Giants game. The towel was dangerously low on his waist. If he moved in just the right way, it could slip off.

And I wanted it to slip off.

I really was a pervert.

I moved into the kitchen and loaded the dishes in the dishwasher, trying to find something else to do other than gawk at my husband next door. It was a huge invasion of privacy, and I felt guilty for even being tempted to look.

But I looked again.

And again.

A commercial must have come on because he walked away and disappeared from my sight.

I returned to the couch and the fire, unable to erase the image from my brain. He was over six feet of pure muscle. I didn't know how he was that ripped because I didn't personally witness him exercise. Complemented by that handsome face and pretty eyes, he was practically a model.

And I was married to him.

I was lonely as hell, and not to mention, horny. The last time I got action I could actually remember was from Cypress, and that was apparently over two years ago. I couldn't find someone else downtown because of my word.

Would it be the end of the world if I slept with him?

After all, I was married to him. I should get something good out of this horrible situation.

But it would lead him on. Even if he'd hurt me, I didn't want to hurt him. Two wrongs didn't make a right.

I kept second-guessing myself, wondering if this was a stupid idea I would regret in the morning.

But I couldn't stop thinking about it. I couldn't stop thinking about how amazing his kisses were, how strong his body felt on top of mine. I was practically salivating like a dog, and that told me I need to get laid.

Like, now.

So I left my house and went next door. He had a gray door without a peephole. My door didn't have one either. I held my fist to the wood but didn't touch it. I lowered my hand again and turned in a circle.

I couldn't do this.

No good would come from it.

I needed to go home and hang out with my vibrator.

The door opened.

God, no.

Cypress stood in sweatpants and a t-shirt, his hair still slightly damp. Even when his hair wasn't done, he was still a perfect ten. He had just shaved his jaw, so his clean look brought out his eyes even more.

How did he know I was there?

"Everything alright, sweetheart?" He opened the door wider, revealing Dino standing behind him, his tongue hanging out like usual.

"How did you know I was here?" I blurted, unable to think of something better to say to explain my random appearance.

"Dino was whining at the door."

"Oh…"

Cypress continued to stare at me, one hand on the doorknob. "Wanna come inside? I've got the game on."

He wasn't going to question why I was there? "Uh, sure."

"Cool." He left the door open and walked into his living room.

Dino jumped on me and pawed at my hips.

"Hey, boy." I kneeled down and gave him a good rubdown, getting a kiss as a thank you. "How are you?"

He barked in response.

"You're so cute." I scratched him behind the ears before I walked into the living room.

Cypress sat on the couch with a beer resting on a coaster. His furniture and home were in light colors, having a distinctly beachy look. Judging from his personality, he had nothing to do with the decoration. "Want a beer?"

"Sure."

He grabbed one from the fridge and popped the lid before he sat down again. "The Giants have had a rough year. Pretty bummed."

The score was obscene. "Man, they got killed."

"Not even sure why I'm watching. Just painful."

Dino jumped on the couch and sat on the other side of me, on a black blanket. I assumed that was his spot since the blanket was there. He looked at me before he closed his eyes, getting comfortable.

"He's had that blanket since the day we got him."

"Yeah?"

"You picked it out at the store." He watched the TV but carried on a conversation with me. "You know, you're welcome to borrow him whenever you want. I take him on a walk in the morning, and you can always tag along."

I patted Dino on the head. "I'll keep that in mind."

Cypress drank his beer and watched the TV like everything was normal. It was the first time I'd been over here since he'd told me the truth about our relationship, and now the place looked totally different. I wondered if I used to come over just to hang out during my eighteen-month hiatus.

He leaned back into the couch with his knees positioned far apart. When I pictured his strong body under those clothes, I wanted to straddle him and ride him right in the living room. I knew exactly what he was packing, and it was every woman's fantasy.

"You want me to get a fire going?" The fireplace was situated underneath the TV in a stone hearth made from Carmel stone. Clint Eastwood owned the quarry, but the precious stone was no longer for sale. It was now a luxury item in the city.

"I'm okay." He drank his beer then set the bottle on the coffee table next to him. He didn't try to make a move or press our relationship at all. He just coexisted with me. "Are you still mad at Ace?"

"No. We buried the hatchet."

"Good. Amelia wouldn't want the two of you to be fighting."

"He apologized, so I forgave him. Amelia is down but not heartbroken, so I let it slide. She's a strong woman. She'll recover."

"I really thought Ace would want to be with her. He was so sprung on her back in the day."

He shrugged. "Things change. People change."

"But Amelia is beautiful. And the girls are adorable."

"Don't worry about her. She'll find a great man soon enough. I have no doubt."

"I've been meaning to track down Evan and give him a piece of my mind..." My palm ached to slap him.

"I already gave him a black eye. I say we forget about that loser."

If I saw him again, I'd slap him anyway.

I pulled on Dino's blanket so I could cover myself with it. "Do you mind sharing?"

The dog scooted closer to me so we could both use the blanket.

"Thanks, Dino." I patted him on the head again, falling in love with this dog I never knew I had. "Does he sleep with you?"

"Yeah. He used to sleep right between us every night. Biggest cockblock I've ever met."

I laughed. "Really?"

"We eventually came up with a routine where we would shut the door, get down to business, and then let him come in the bedroom when we were finished."

I laughed again. "Aww...he just likes to be with us."

"A little too much. But he really helped me after the accident. I was sleeping alone every night, and he kept me company. Wouldn't have known what to do without him."

I looked at Cypress and felt the ache in my chest. If the situation had been reversed and I'd lost the man I loved, I wouldn't be able to get out of bed. When I caught Cypress cheating on me, I was a wreck for a solid three months. "I'm glad he was there for you."

"He's a good boy."

Cypress and I enjoyed each other's company as we watched the rest of the game. We were alone together in the house, and I kept thinking about how satisfying it would feel to have amazing sex that night. But I didn't make a move because it seemed wrong, like I would be crossing a line I had drawn.

The game ended at nine in the evening. I should go to bed soon and so should he since we both would be up early in the morning. But I stayed put, unsure how I wanted to play this. Having an honest conversation seemed like the best move. "I'm horny."

He turned to me, an attractive smile on his lips.

My cheeks reddened at my poor tactic. "That didn't come out right..."

"I think it came out perfect." He set his beer down and rested his arm over the back of the couch. Now that he knew what I wanted, he came close to me and moved his hand to my thigh.

I grabbed his wrist and steadied it. "I just want sex. I haven't been with anyone in a long time, and it's not like I can go out and find someone..."

"That's fine with me."

"It doesn't mean we're getting back together."

"I understand, sweetheart." He moved into me again.

I pulled away. "I just don't want to lead you on."

"Listen to me." He moved his hand to my cheek, and he rested his thumb in the corner of my mouth. "I've been married to you for two years, and I've gotten laid, maybe, twenty times in the past eighteen months. I'm a very sexual guy, and I've been extremely frustrated living next door to my gorgeous wife without being able to fuck her. If you wanna use me, please do. I want you to."

With his hand on my cheek and the scorching look in his eyes, I melted. I didn't want to argue anymore or talk about the meaning of our actions. I wanted to feel his body everywhere, grip his ass, and pull him farther into me. I wanted to feel like a woman, to have this beautiful man want me with every fiber of his being.

Cypress moved in and kissed me, and this time, I didn't stop him. His kiss was soft despite the passion raging through both of us. His hand snaked around my neck, and he lowered me to the couch as the kiss continued.

It was exactly as I remembered it, but better.

We moved on top of Dino, and when Dino got too uncomfortable, he hopped off the couch and jumped into the armchair closest to the fireplace.

Cypress wrapped one leg around my waist and ground his cock into me, pressing his erection right against my denim-covered clit.

Even that felt good.

My hands slid up his shirt and felt the individual muscles of his body. I loved feeling the hardness, the concrete. My nails pressed lightly into the skin, feeling the muscles shift every time he moved. When I reached his shoulders, I grabbed on to him and held on, feeling his chest press against mine. He was so heavy and dense, and I liked being pinned down by his size and strength.

He parted my mouth with his and kissed me harder, his lips nearly trembling in passion. When he gave me his tongue, I moaned into his mouth, burned by the charge between us. The electricity sparked and warmed both of us.

His hand slid underneath my t-shirt, and he gripped my tit through my bra, squeezing me hard and making me wince under the force of his powerful fingertips.

My hands yanked on his shirt until it was over his head. He pulled it the rest of the way off and tossed it somewhere in the living room, probably landing on the hardwood floor.

I broke our kiss just to look at him, to see that powerful physique I'd gawked at almost every day. My fingers ran down his hard chest and over his chiseled eight-pack, and eventually, his thin happy trail that led into his sweatpants.

I gripped the top of his sweatpants and pulled them down along with his boxers, watching his hard cock emerge. It was exactly as I remembered it, nine inches of thickness that made my lips part and my tongue press against the back of my teeth.

I pulled his bottoms below his ass, but I couldn't reach any farther. His cock hung out as well as his balls. I remembered sucking both into my mouth countless times and thoroughly enjoying it.

Cypress kicked everything off until it was shoved into the cushions of the couch. Now he was totally naked—and beautiful.

He got off the couch and pulled me with him. At six three, he towered over me by a foot. When he looked down at me, he wore an expression a king might give to his queen, of complete ownership. Without warning, he scooped me up off my feet and carried me down the hallway. Before Dino could get into the bedroom, Cypress shut the door with his foot then set me on the bed.

I loved being carried like that. And I loved that he was strong enough to do it without effort.

His bedroom matched his personality better, dark colors with dark furniture. The shade was pulled down, so we were enveloped in complete darkness. But I did notice the picture frame on his nightstand.

It was a picture of me and Dino.

We were sitting on the beach together, looking out at the water. It seemed candid, and as if neither one of us knew our picture was being taken.

He watched me glance at it before he unbuttoned my jeans and pulled them off. He slid them to my ankles then kneeled down to get them off the rest of the way. Even when he was on the floor, his eyes were focused on mine. With every movement he made, his beautiful physique shifted and remained tight.

He grabbed my thong next and pulled it down my thighs and over my knees. When my bottom was bare, he stared at my pussy like it was the sexiest thing he'd ever seen. His eyes narrowed with intensity before he gripped my hips and yanked me to the edge of the bed, causing my upper body to fall back on the covers.

He sealed his mouth over me and kissed me, his tongue swirling around my sensitive nub like this wasn't his first rodeo. He sucked and kissed me, lavishing my lips aggressively. He blew on my nub before he kissed me again.

I forgot how good he was at that. My hands dug into my hair as I lost my mind with lust. I panted and moaned, writhing uncontrollably. He was going to make me come like this. I didn't even need him inside me.

He pulled away just before I plummeted into the abyss of pleasure.

"Cypress..."

He yanked my shirt off my head and nearly ripped my bra as he got it off. Then he laid me back as he got on top of me, his cock throbbing as he rubbed it against my soaked entrance. He tilted his hips and pressed his head inside my wetness.

I wanted all of him right then and there. But there was still a small piece of logic inside me. "Condom."

He didn't get off me. "You have an IUD."

"That doesn't protect from other things." I didn't want to talk about it. I just wanted him to get that condom on so he could fuck me.

"Sweetheart, I'm clean."

"Well, I don't trust you, so put something on."

His eyes fell in offense.

He claimed he'd been faithful to me for the past eighteen months, but I didn't know if I could believe that. I didn't retain any memories of that time, so he may have brought tons of women over, and I never would know about it. When it came to my health, I'd rather be safe than sorry. "You either put on a condom, or this isn't happening."

He sighed then got off me. He opened his nightstand, pulled out a foil packet, and then rolled the latex onto his dick.

Some of my arousal had disappeared after having that awkward conversation, but he looked so hot rolling the condom onto his huge dick that I got right back in the mood.

I moved onto my stomach, holding myself up on my hands and knees.

The bed sank when Cypress moved his knees onto the bed. He positioned himself behind me then pressed his cock inside my soaked entrance. His fingers dug into my hips, and he slowly pulled me down onto his length.

"Oh god..." I closed my eyes and melted at the feeling of his thick cock. He was so hard that it made me feel even more desirable.

He released a quiet groan once every inch of his length was inside me. "Sweetheart...your pussy is amazing." He positioned himself right against me before he thrust hard, moving his entire length inside me. He wasn't gentle or easy. He fucked me just the way I wanted, pounding into me and making the headboard clap against the wall. His hips moved faster than I could fathom, and he plowed me into an orgasm that was so good, it was practically violent.

My face hit the comforter, and I cried into the mattress, enjoying the best orgasm I'd felt in forever. Cypress's hand was on the back of my neck, and he kept me down as he finished, moaning and groaning until he filled the tip of the condom. "Fuck." His fingers gripped my neck even tighter as he finished.

I closed my eyes and felt my lungs work to fill my blood with oxygen because I was still out of breath. Now that I was utterly satisfied, I just wanted to go to sleep. My body was exhausted, and I was grateful I only had to make it next door.

Cypress finally pulled out of me and cleaned up in the bathroom. When he returned, he lay on the bed beside me and cuddled into my side.

I still hadn't opened my eyes, and I felt for his body without sight. I got comfortable in the crook of his arm with my thigh wrapped around his leg. I could easily fall asleep like that, but I knew it wasn't a good idea. That would cross a line I wasn't ready for. "I should go..." I moved from his embrace and went to stand up.

"Stay." He pulled me back into his side and pressed a kiss to my forehead.

The fact that his kiss felt good told me I needed to go. "No. I told you I just wanted sex—nothing more."

He squeezed me a bit harder before he finally released me.

I pulled my clothes on without looking at him, avoiding the disappointment in his eyes.

After a sigh, he got up and pulled on his clothes so he could walk me to the door. Dino accompanied us, trailing behind on our way to the front of the house.

He got the door open then looked at me. "You know I'm always available." He leaned in.

I knew he was going to kiss me, but I didn't stop it. I felt his mouth on mine and kissed him back, feeling the same warmth in my belly as I had earlier. "Good night."

"Good night." He smiled before he let me go. "I'll see you in the morning."

I walked back to my house, doing the walk of shame for twenty feet until I was back in the privacy of my home. When I went to close the shades in the living room, I spotted Cypress sitting on his couch again. Another beer was on the coffee table, and Dino was resting his chin on Cypress's thigh. Cypress petted him with one hand as he kept his eyes on the screen. Like he knew I was watching him, he turned my way and looked at me.

I held his gaze and suddenly felt lonely again. I wanted to be in that living room with him, living the life we should have had. If he hadn't cheated on me, I'd be happy right now. I'd have a handsome husband who was also sweet and devoted. I would have my dog on my lap with the fire roaring in the hearth.

But I didn't have any of that.

20

AMELIA

I held Rose's hand as Bree held Lily's. I had a backpack over my shoulders stuffed with the sand toys, and when we reached the volleyball courts, they would immediately get to work on building sand castles.

The guys walked behind us, Cypress with the ball tucked under his arm.

"Do anything fun last night?" I asked.

Bree immediately smiled, the kind of grin that reached her eyes. "No."

There was no way she actually thought I believed her. "Spill it."

She nodded behind us, where Cypress was walking. "Later."

"Ooh...I want all the details."

We reached the volleyball nets at the top of the sand hill right before the beach. The back corner one was open, so we set up in the sand. The girls took off their dresses and sat in their bathing suits. They immediately got to work with the shovels and buckets and tried to make something.

"What are the teams?" Blade asked.

"Bree, Amelia, and me versus you two." Cypress stripped off his shirt and dropped it on his backpack. He was in his dark green swim trunks, and his body looked magnificent under the California sun. I knew he was my brother-in-law, but I'd have to be blind to say he wasn't hot as hell.

Blade took off his shirt next. "Fine by me." He was muscular too, showing off an eight-pack that rivaled Cypress's. His skin was a shade darker from running along the beach in the morning.

Ace came next. I shouldn't be surprised by what I saw, but of course, I was.

He was so damn fine.

Rock-hard pecs, strong abdomen, and a definitive V along his hips. His arms were cut, chiseled with a butcher knife, and his chin was marked with facial hair because he'd skipped the shave for the last few days.

Damn, I wish he wanted me.

Being fuck buddies didn't sound so bad right now. With that body on top of mine every night, I wouldn't utter a single complaint.

Ace turned to me, and his mouth moved.

Shit, did he say something? "Uh…what?"

"Do you want to play with us?" he repeated. If he knew I was gawking at him, he pretended he didn't.

"No, I'm gonna stay with the girls." If I was sitting on the sidelines, I got to stare at his perfect body the entire time. Sounded like a great way to spend the evening, if you asked me.

"I'll swap you after this game." Ace stood behind the sand line and served the ball.

They were all pretty good and kept the ball moving. Bree lagged behind a little, but that didn't surprise me because the guys were simply more athletic than she was. I knew Cypress woke up at the crack of dawn every morning to work out. Ace hit the gym twice day. I didn't have a clue how he found the time.

A group of women walked past in their bikinis, and they eyed the guys like candy.

Blade was the only one to look back.

Cypress didn't seem to notice they were there.

Ace didn't either.

The girls kept walking and moved down the hill.

Looking at the women made me think of Lady. I wondered if she was coming. Ace seemed to invite her to a lot of things. He claimed it wasn't serious, but he spent a lot of time with her. She was a nice person, but since she was a major conflict of interest, I would never like her.

After the game ended, Ace walked over to me. "Swap me."

"No, it's okay," I said. "But thank you."

"Come on." He extended his hand to help me up, a smile on his lips. "You don't need to be a mom all the time."

I didn't want to be a mom all the time. I wanted to be so much more. I grabbed his wrist, and he pulled me up. He jerked me a little hard, and I bumped into his chest on the way up.

I had to stop myself from kissing him. My mouth was near his, and it would be so easy. I didn't even care if my daughters witnessed it. Now that I'd had him once before,

I wanted him again. He was the best sex I'd ever had. Evan couldn't hold a candle to Ace's performance.

Ace must have felt the energy between us because he cleared his throat and stepped away, dropping his smile and good mood. "Girls, you wanna head to the beach? It'd be a lot easier to build the sand castles with water."

"Yeah!" Rose jumped up and hugged him around the waist. "Thank, Uncle Ace."

I rolled my eyes. "They act like I don't do anything for them."

Ace chuckled. "You know they love you." He walked with them down the hill to the water's edge.

I walked onto the court and stood beside Blade. "Why does he have to be so hot?"

"Ace?" he asked.

"Who else do you think I'm talking about?"

"Uh, me?" Blade asked. "Obviously."

"Why would I talk about you in the third person?"

He shrugged. "Maybe you're a little embarrassed? I don't know."

"Well, I wasn't."

"I guess I have to admit Ace is pretty hot. If I were a woman, I'd probably ask him out."

Cypress put his hands on his hips as he stared down his friend. "Dude, I'm worried about you."

"What?" Blade said. "If you were a woman, you wouldn't want to go out with Ace?"

"I'm not a woman. I'm a man. And hell no."

"Oh, come on," Blade said. "He's built like a brickhouse. Chicks dig that."

"I don't care what chicks dig," Cypress said. "Are we gonna play or what?"

"Fine, whatever," Blade said. "Serve the damn ball."

I walked down to the beach when the game was over. Ace had helped them build one of the biggest sand castles I'd ever seen. They formed a system like worker ants. The girls retrieved the water and made the foundation for the next part. Ace used shovels and spoons to carve out the intricate details out of the outside.

"Wow. That's a pretty awesome sand castle."

He hadn't realized I was there because he was focused on what he was doing. "Thanks. The girls are doing a great job."

Rose came back with another pail of water. "Here's another one, Uncle Ace."

"Thanks, kiddo." Ace took the water and molded the last structure of the castle. He dumped the remaining water out then carved out the windows and doorway.

"Isn't it cool, Mommy?" Lily asked. She wrapped herself in her beach towel because the sun was going down and it had started to get chilly.

"Very cool," I said. "You guys are so creative."

"Uncle Ace did most of it," Rose said. "But we helped."

"You helped a lot." Ace got to his feet and stood back to admire his handiwork. "Now, that's a pretty sick castle."

"We love it!" Lily clapped her hands.

Ace dug into his pocket and pulled out his phone. "Amy, could you take a picture of us?"

"Sure." I took the phone from him and stood back, getting Ace and the girls in the picture along with the sand castle. Ace wrapped his arms around the girls and smiled for the camera.

I took a few photos and felt my heart melt when I looked at them. I quickly texted them to myself, wanting to print them out and put them in a frame for the living room. "That was a lot of fun, but we should get going."

"What about our sand castle?" Lily asked. "Can we take it with us?"

Ace chuckled. "No, kiddo. But we have a picture so we can look at it forever."

They packed up their stuff in their backpack then handed it to me.

"I can take that." Ace took it from Rose and put it over his shoulders.

"That's sweet, but I can handle it." I'd developed muscular arms ever since I had my girls. I had to carry them, load their car seats, pack strollers, the whole nine yards.

"Forget it." Ace started walking toward the hill.

"Are you going to say goodbye to your friends?" Rose asked as she looked over at the group of women I saw earlier.

Ace waved.

The women smiled and waved back.

I didn't have any right to be jealous, so I didn't get jealous. I just let it go. But I wondered if he'd gotten a phone number while I was busy playing volleyball. Since I didn't want to know, I didn't ask.

We walked up the hill and met the rest of the gang at the top.

"Are we doing anything else?" Blade asked.

"I should get the girls home. They need to get cleaned up and have some dinner," I said.

"Alright," Blade said. "I'm stopping by 400 Degrees Burgers than heading home."

Cypress glanced at Bree, silently asking her what she wanted to do.

That had to be an indication something serious happened last night. She must have slept with him. It wouldn't be the first time.

"We'll come along," Bree answered. "What about you, Ace?"

"I'm gonna help Amelia get the girls home," he said. "I'll see you tomorrow."

Help me get the girls home? I didn't need any help. "That's really okay, Ace. Don't worry about it."

"Too bad," he said with a smile. "I'm walking you home."

Bree shot a glance at me, her meaning crystal clear. It was a sister thing.

I didn't argue further. "Okay."

We went our separate ways, and Ace and I walked to my house on Monte Verde. I lived close to Mission Ranch, a hotel and restaurant that was still owned by the famous Clint Eastwood. He also had been the mayor of the town at one point, long before my time.

Instead of holding my hand like she usually did, Rose grabbed Ace's hand. He looked down at her touch but didn't make a comment about it, taking the affection in stride.

Lily held my hand and stuck close to my side.

Seeing us together like this made me think of things I shouldn't. Ace was so good with my girls, and he was such a great guy too. I'd be lucky to have him, but he simply wanted something else. I couldn't blame him for that, but moments like this made me sad. I'd need to start dating someone so I could rule out the possibility of Ace and me ever having any kind of future.

He was so hot and sweet at the same time. Absolutely perfect. But that told me he was too good to be true.

He walked into the house and set our shoes by the door. "You guys get ready to take a bath. I'll be there in a second."

They both walked down the hallway, still in their swimsuits.

Ace stood by the door and set down the backpack. "You're a good mom, Amelia. Just want you to know that."

Every mother lived to hear those words, approval that she was doing something right. "Thanks…"

"I know it hasn't been all fun and games for you, but you make it look easy."

Again, another compliment that went straight to my heart. "Thanks."

"You want me to pick up some dinner?" he asked.

"No, you've done enough." I couldn't take advantage of his chivalry. I was sure he had something more interesting to do tonight. "I can always throw some pizza bagels in the oven, and they'll be happy."

"Alright. You know where to find me if you change your mind." He walked to the door, his shirt back on so his muscles were hidden from view.

I walked him to the entryway and kept a smile on my lips, not wanting him to know how sad I was every time he left.

He crossed the threshold, turned around, and looked at me.

"Well, I'll see you later."

He slid his hands into his pockets and tilted his head slightly. "Yeah…I'll see you later."

"Good night."

He didn't say it back, choosing to stare at me instead.

I held my breath as I waited for him to say something in return, to change his mind about what we'd agreed on.

For the most part, the awkwardness disappeared and our friendship returned to normal, but I couldn't stop thinking about how great we were together. I couldn't stop thinking about how explosive our kisses were. I wished he would make love to me like that every single night.

But he didn't say any of that. "Good night." He turned around and walked away.

Maybe he wasn't thinking of saying anything in the first place. Maybe something else was on his mind. Maybe he wanted to ask if it would be weird if he started bringing Lady around again. Whatever the case, I didn't want to get my hopes up. More than likely, I was overthinking it.

And I would just be disappointed.

"ARE YOU GOING TO TELL ME WHAT HAPPENED OR NOT?" The only place I could talk to Bree without Cypress knowing about it was at the Hippopotamus Café. He usually spent his day focused on the other restaurants since Bree handled this place on her own.

We sat at a table in one of the alcoves, having lunch together while the employees carried on. Bree sipped her iced tea then glanced around as if Cypress were going to pop out of nowhere. "So...we slept together."

"That's great." I wanted my sister to get back together with Cypress as much as Cypress did. Knowing what their marriage had been like convinced me she was supposed to be with him and not anyone else. But I could never influence her like that. "So, you guys are working on the marriage?"

"No...it was just a hookup."

"Oh..." I didn't think Bree would do something like that under the circumstances.

"I told him I wouldn't divorce him, and I would keep an open mind for the next seven months. But I can't not get laid. I need some action. And since he's the only one I can be with...I asked if he wanted to hook up."

Of course, Cypress would never turn down the opportunity. "How was it?"

"Amazing, like always."

"Are you going to do it again?"

"I don't know...probably. But only once in a while. I don't want it to be a regular thing. I'll get trapped."

Maybe sleeping with him would bring them closer together. Sex certainly complicated things. "I think you should keep hooking up with him. I mean, you're married to him, right? May as well take advantage of it."

"True. But I'm not sure how I feel about the whole thing. There are times when I think he's really sweet and I can see us making it work. But then there are times when I wonder if he's lying to me."

"Lying to you about what?"

"For instance, he said he didn't want to use a condom. He said he's clean and hasn't been with anyone else for the past year and a half. But can I really trust that?"

There wasn't a doubt in my mind that Cypress remained faithful to her—always. But I couldn't hold it against her for having doubts. She had every right to feel that way. "I see what you mean."

"I feel like I go back and forth a lot. I don't mean to. Just happens."

"You've only had your memory back for six weeks. It's gonna take a lot longer than that to be certain of what you want."

"Yeah, probably." She sipped her iced tea and then tilted her head to the side. "It seems like Ace pays a lot of attention to you..."

"He's always been that way."

"Yeah, but I see him stare at you all the time."

She had no idea how much I wished that were true. "It doesn't mean anything. Ace could have me whenever he wanted me, but he doesn't. If he did, he would have said something."

"Maybe he's thinking about it."

I shrugged. "He said he just wants to be friends, so I'm gonna assume that's how he feels."

"He's so sweet to you and the girls."

"But he was like that before."

"Well, keep this in mind," she said. "He's never been that sweet to me. I'm not complaining, but he obviously feels differently toward you than he does for everyone else. I think there's a chance."

"Well, I'm pretty sure he got some woman's number at the beach. And he's still seeing Lady. So...I'm not getting my hopes up."

"Hmm...maybe he cares more about being a manwhore than being with a good woman."

I shrugged. "That's what Cypress says."

"I'm sorry, Amelia. Maybe he'll come around."

I found that unlikely. "The girls asked for Evan yesterday." I didn't want to talk about this, but it was gnawing at me.

"They did?" She abandoned her iced tea altogether and gave me all her focus.

"Yeah. Rose said she misses Daddy. Lily asked when he was coming back." I hated my ex-husband so much. I could forgive him for cheating and leaving me, but I couldn't forgive him for letting down our girls. It was unacceptable. He had no idea how it was on them. "I'm afraid they're going to grow up thinking their father doesn't love them…that messes people up."

Bree lowered her head and sighed under her breath. "Maybe you should talk to him. Put his head on straight."

"I hate talking to him."

"I know," she said gently. "But for the girls."

"I've tried before."

"I'm more than happy to do it for you. And I'm sure Cypress is too."

That wouldn't get me anywhere. "No, it's hostile if it comes from anyone else. I need to do it."

She rested her hand on mine. "I'm so sorry, Amelia. I wish none of this had ever happened."

"One out of two marriages ends in divorce. I'm fine with that. But why can't we still be a family?" I wanted to break down in tears right then and there, but I refused to let that happen. Crying wouldn't get me anywhere. And a pity party was certainly a terrible idea.

"There's no reason why you can't. Talk to him again. Fight for your girls."

I would always fight for them—because they were my whole world.

It wasn't the ideal time to call, but I waited until the girls were asleep before I picked up the phone and dialed his number. He was probably lying next to that stupid whore who was barely an adult right then.

It rang three times.

Then he answered. "Everything alright?"

Was that concern he showed? I didn't think he possessed such a thing. Instead of making a sarcastic comment, I pushed through. "Everything is fine. You haven't come by to see the girls in a long time, and they miss you."

Silence.

He was part of their lives for so long, and now he didn't care? What kind of person did something like that? He'd spent holidays and birthdays with them, and now they were just a thing of the past—like I was.

"They said that?" he whispered.

"Of course. You haven't seen them in four months. They want to see you, Evan."

I could hear whispers over the line. His new girlfriend was saying something, but I couldn't make out what it was. He said something back, and I couldn't decipher that either. Then the sound of shuffling erupted as he left the room to get some privacy.

"Everything okay?" I asked.

"Yeah," he said. "I'm not sure when I'm gonna have time to stop by. I'll let you know."

"Not sure when you'll have time…?" Now I wanted to scream at the top of my lungs. "Evan, these are your daughters."

"I know, I know," he said quickly. "I've just been busy—"

"How busy can you be? I work full time and then come home to them every night. You don't have a legitimate excuse at all."

Silence.

"Is it because of her?" I didn't even want to consider the possibility that this woman was purposely keeping him from his kids. That was a new form of evil I didn't know existed.

Evan never answered my question. "I should get going. It's late."

"Evan, your daughters are asking to see you. They're gonna get older, and when they do, they'll hate you. I don't want that to happen—"

"Why are you still on the phone?" Her catty voice came over the line loud and clear.

"I gotta go," Evan said.

"Wait—"

He hung up.

The son of a bitch hung up on me.

I tossed the phone on the table, about to give in to the grief that was sweeping through me. Tears burned in my eyes, and they couldn't be stopped. I let them fall down my cheeks, streaking to my lips.

I was so disappointed in him.

I didn't ask for a single thing from him, not even child support anymore. All I wanted was for him to be a father. That was it.

I wanted to call Bree so she could calm me down, but I didn't know if she was busy with Cypress. I wanted them to work it out. Cypress would never do something like this to her. Maybe he'd cheated on her a long time ago, but Cypress was a changed man. Evan never cheated on me in the past, but when the right woman came along, he turned into the biggest asshole on the planet.

Without thinking, I called Ace.

"Hey, what's going on?" He answered on the first ring, his voice attractive and charming.

The tears kept falling from my eyes. "I'm sorry to bother you…"

Ace's attitude completely changed when he heard the sound of my voice. "What is it, baby? Talk to me."

"I talked to Evan..."

The sound of movement erupted over the phone. "I'm on my way, okay? I'll be there in five minutes."

"You don't have to come over—"

"I'll be there in five minutes. Now keep talking to me."

I couldn't get my ex-husband to spend time with our kids, but Ace jumped to my aid the second he heard my distress. "I told him the girls needed him, but he wasn't responsive. What's-Her-Name told him to get off the phone. I think she doesn't want him to see the girls."

"Are you serious?" he asked. "What kind of psychopath would do that?"

"I don't know..."

"I need to kick his ass."

"That won't do anything. I just don't want my girls to hate him, you know? He's their father."

"Honestly, they should hate him. What kind of man leaves his wife for a woman ten years younger than him? What kind of man abandons his kids? He's not a good role model for them, and if that's how he's gonna be, then good riddance. They've got you, me, Cypress, Bree, and Blade. They've got all the family they need."

I started to cry harder because those words meant everything to me.

My front door opened and closed when he arrived. He hung up the phone and shoved it into his pocket before he pulled up a chair and sat in front of me in the kitchen. He watched the tears stream down my face before he moved me into his lap and wrapped his arms around my waist.

I rested my face in the crook of his neck, grateful for the privacy he gave me. I cried my eyes out as he held me against his chest, his strong arms protecting me from everything in the outside world. I felt weak for breaking down like this, but I couldn't stay strong anymore. The loneliness wasn't so bad. The emptiness wasn't so bad either. But knowing my girls didn't have a father killed me inside. I wanted them to feel only loved—never anything else. "I'm sorry..."

"Why are you apologizing to me?" He moved his hand through my hair.

"For crying...for bothering you."

"You never bother me, Amelia. I'm here because I want to be here. I play with your girls because I think they're angels. Don't ever think otherwise."

"I just feel weak for letting him get to me like this. When he left, I told myself I wouldn't cry over him again."

"You aren't crying for him." His hand trailed down my back. "You're crying for your daughters. Being sad doesn't make us weak. It's okay to collapse. But it's not okay not to get back up again. I know you'll get back up stronger than you were before. But you need to cry for now."

I clung to him tighter, grateful he was there. "You're such a sweetheart, Ace..." My feelings for him had never been only superficial. They went way beyond skin deep, recognizing his kind soul and his good heart. When he found the right woman, he would be a great father and husband. He would never let his family feel the way I did now.

"I'm a sweetheart for you, Amelia." He turned his face into mine so he could meet my gaze.

My eyes were red and wet, but I managed to make myself stop crying. I held his look, my lips trembling and my body weak. He made my heart soar high above the clouds. He made me feel stronger than I really was. My body succumbed to his handsomeness, but my heart was even weaker for his.

His hand moved into my hair, and he turned my face toward his, his fingers hinting at the strength he possessed. If I'd wanted to move away, he wouldn't have allowed me. He would have kept me in place as long as he wished. He pressed his forehead to mine, and his warm breath moved across my lips.

The tears halted immediately. I couldn't even breathe. He hadn't kissed me, but I felt all the emotions that overtook me when he did.

His thumb swiped the corner of my mouth before he kissed me, his lips soft and delicate as they caressed mine. He'd never kissed me this gently before, treating me like I was made of glass.

I closed my eyes and kissed him back. My arms circled his neck tighter, and I pressed my body into him, my nipples hard and poking into my cotton bra. Instead of pulling away, I let the emotions and hormones get to me. I moved my mouth harder against his, pulling his bottom lip into my mouth. He was such an incredible kisser that I didn't think about Evan or the stupid bimbo he left me for. I just thought about Ace.

Within a minute, I felt his erection through his jeans. Thick and impressive, his package pressed right against the most sensitive part between my legs. The tears I'd shed had long disappeared, dissolving into my skin and his fingertips, and now I could only think about having that enormous dick inside me. Every touch was sensual, and I wanted my heart to be touched in the same way. I didn't think about any consequences that would transpire in the morning. It had been a mistake the first time, and it would be a mistake the second time as well.

But that didn't stop me.

My hands reached to the top of his fly, and I unbuttoned his jeans.

His lips hesitated as he kissed me, but once the zipper was down and his boxers were exposed, he kissed me harder than before. His tongue swiped against mine in an erotic dance, and I felt my panties dampen in preparation.

Ace rose to his feet and carried me with him effortlessly. His hands slid under my ass, and he kept me right against his chest before he moved through the living room and into the hallway.

My arms tightened around his neck, and I held myself up as much as possible even though he could handle my weight without a struggle. He carried me into my bedroom, which was down the hallway from the one the girls shared. He gently shut the door behind him rather than kick it closed and then laid me on the bed, his body falling with me.

Clothes came off, and the kisses turned dangerous. He kissed my neck and groped my tits as he kicked his jeans and boxers away. Once our clothes were gone and we were naked, he positioned himself on top of me. "Got a condom?"

All the joy left my body when I realized there wasn't a single one in the house. Evan and I never used them, and I hadn't been with anyone else since he left. I'd had an IUD placed inside me after Lily was born because Evan and I agreed we didn't want more than two kids. "No..."

He pressed his lips to mine but didn't kiss me. A restrained sigh came from his lips. "I'm clean." He looked to me for permission, leaving the ball in my court. "Never been with a woman without wearing one." He didn't ask if

I was clean in return, probably because the answer was obvious.

Ace wouldn't lie to me, especially about something like health. "I have an IUD."

"Is that a yes?" he whispered.

I wanted to feel Ace's come inside me. Just thinking about it made my nipples harden. "Yes."

He dug his hand into my hair, and he kissed me with the same forceful sensuality as before. Instead of the conversation ruining the mood, it seemed to invigorate it. He wrapped my legs around his waist before he slid inside me, moving through my overwhelming slickness with a swift thrust. "Fuck..." He kept his voice low, but it was a struggle. His hand tightened on my hair, and he yanked on my scalp slightly.

I loved feeling his bare skin without latex between us. It felt incredible, skin-to-skin. My ankles locked together, and I gripped the back of his shoulders like last time, holding on for the ride that was about to commence.

He didn't fuck me with the same momentum as last time. My girls were in the same house, so we couldn't make a sound. The headboard couldn't tap against the wall, and I couldn't scream when he made me come.

But the restrained silence somehow made it hotter. We breathed against each other's mouths and struggled to remain quiet even though it felt so good. My nails dug into his back, nearly drawing blood, and I had to swallow all the moans that formed on the back of my tongue. Somehow, it was better than last time.

"Amelia..."

I panted into his mouth when I heard him say my name. He made me feel like a beautiful woman, the one he spotted across the room and needed to have. When his cock was that thick because of me, I felt more beautiful than I did on my wedding day.

With a few more thrusts, I came, crushing my mouth against his so I wouldn't shout loudly like I did last time. I forced myself to remain quiet, even biting my bottom lip just to make sure nothing escaped my throat. My channel tightened around his cock, and I could feel my come sheathe him all the way to his balls.

"Fuck." He looked into my eyes as he came, the sexiest expression I'd ever seen him wear. He shoved the head of his cock all the way to my cervix as he released, filling me with mounds of arousal. His eyes darkened and his jaw clenched.

Now I was turned on all over again.

He ended his thrusts and remained on top of me, buried inside me along with all the come he'd just given me.

I didn't want him to pull out. I didn't want him to leave. "Fuck me again."

He gave me a soft kiss. "I'll fuck you all night."

I walked Ace to the door at four in the morning. We slept for a few hours, but we both agreed he should be out of the house before the girls woke up. I didn't want to be stuck explaining Ace's presence to a seven- and five-year-old. I also didn't want them to get used to another man who wouldn't be sticking around.

I didn't know what this hook up meant for us, but my expectations were low. When he came over, I wasn't looking for sex and neither was he. It kinda just happened. It might have happened sooner if we were ever alone together. I felt the attraction pull on both of us whenever we were near each other.

We stepped outside into the darkness and shut the door behind us.

Ace turned to me, his hair messy and his eyes heavy-lidded with exhaustion.

I didn't know what to say, so I let him speak first.

"I'm sorry."

That was the last thing I expected him to say. "What?"

"I'm sorry I kissed you. I'm sorry this happened."

There was nothing to be sorry about. "I'm not. I really enjoyed it."

A ghost of a smile stretched on his lips. "I did too. But Cypress is right, it's wrong."

"Nothing that good is wrong."

"Well, it can't happen again. When I came over here, I genuinely wanted to comfort you."

"I never doubted that, Ace." I crossed my arms over my chest, feeling cold the second his arms weren't wrapped around me. "Don't feel bad about it. If you hadn't initiated it, I probably would have."

He bowed his head and nodded. "Can we keep this between us?"

I knew Ace wasn't looking for anything serious, and tonight wouldn't change that, but I still couldn't swallow the disappointment all the way down. I wished we could have sex like that every night. I wished I could always sleep full of his come. "Of course."

"Alright. Cypress would kill me if he knew."

"Cypress is just overprotective."

"Well, he has every right to be." Ace stepped closer to me and wrapped his arm around my waist. "Good night."

"Good night." I braced myself for the kiss that would make me feel numb everywhere.

And it did. He kissed me softly before he pulled away. "See you in a few hours."

"Okay." I watched him go, wearing a smile that wasn't truly genuine. I was happy I got to spend the evening with him, but I was sad I wouldn't get to spend tomorrow night with him. I would be alone in my bed.

Thinking about him.

21

BREE

The sun was out when I walked out the front door that morning. A white envelope sat on the doormat. I picked it up and saw my name scribbled on the front in masculine handwriting. The envelope was sealed, so I used my finger to rip it open.

Inside were test results.

Cypress's STD results.

He was clean.

Cypress walked out of his house, obviously spotting me through his front windows. He was in jeans and a long-sleeve t-shirt with a cleanly shaven jaw. His blue eyes matched the beautiful sky that was free of all clouds. "You got my letter."

I glanced at the letter one more time before I tossed it inside on the entry table and shut the door behind me. "Yes." I didn't lock the door behind me because that was something I never did. Crime was nonexistent in a small town like this.

Cypress stood at the end of my stone steps, looking

handsome with that charming smile he possessed. "Hope it was an interesting read."

I stopped myself from rolling my eyes as I walked down the steps. "A little."

"Now that we've got that out of the way, we shouldn't have to wear anything next time." He started walking, his powerful arms swinging by his sides.

"Why would that change anything?" I walked beside him and placed my hands in the pockets of my jacket.

He looked down at me. "It says I'm clean. As in, I don't have anything to give you."

"At the time you took that test, yes."

"Which was forty-eight hours ago. It's not like I slipped you an old test."

"But I don't know what you're doing when I'm not around." I didn't mean to put him down or make him feel worse than he already did, but I was being honest.

"Oh, come on." He rubbed his temple and sighed. "I can understand your insecurity for the past eighteen months, but you really think I'm gonna fuck someone when I'm trying to make us work?"

"You fucked someone else when we were happy. So why not?" Bitterness flooded my mouth because I wasn't over what happened. I forgave him, but it was nearly impossible for me to trust him again. Sometimes my anger was under control, but other times, it slipped out.

He clenched his jaw at the jab, his entire body tense. "You work with me and live next door to me. You know where I am at all hours of the day."

"All you have to do is text one of your bimbos when I'm asleep. I'd never know."

"I would never do that, Bree. And in your heart, you know that's true."

"Why would I know that?" I demanded. "When we were together, I was so head over heels for you that I actually thought we would get married. I even told Amelia you were my future husband—"

"And you were right."

"I was dead wrong."

"No, you weren't. I made a mistake, and I'm not that guy anymore. Not once did I make an excuse for my behavior. I've owned up to it honestly. I'll never hide anything from you."

"Good to know. So next time you cheat, you'll let me know."

He sighed again, his anger growing. "I'll never hurt you again. I give you my word."

His word was worthless. I turned onto 7th and walked uphill. We were ruining the beautiful day with this stupid fight. "You already gave me your word once before, Cypress."

He finally lost his temper. "Then what the hell do I have to do so you stop assuming I'll fuck anything that walks by?"

"I don't know. What did you do last time?"

He moved his hands into his pockets as he walked beside me.

"What did you do?" I repeated.

"I just didn't give up…"

"Well, good luck with that." Didn't seem like we were gonna make too many changes. Even if his test results were negative, I wasn't eager to reward him with any kind of trust. He might be hot and sweet, but I wasn't willing to catch something just because I let my guard down sooner than I should.

"What happened to forgiving me?"

"I did forgive you."

"Doesn't seem like it."

"I just don't trust you, Cypress. If I hadn't forgiven you, I wouldn't have slept with you."

We walked the rest of the way in silence, Cypress finally giving up on the argument. We stepped into the office above Amelia's Place a few minutes later. It was just the two of us, and I was acutely aware of the fact that there were no witnesses. Apparently, we used to fuck on his desk all the time.

I sat down and found something to do before my café opened. Cypress sat at his own desk and looked out the window, watching the breeze move gently through the leaves.

A few minutes later, Ace walked inside. He rubbed the sleep from his eyes and yawned loudly, looking half asleep as he staggered into the room. His clothes weren't as crisp as they usually were, and it didn't seem like he'd bothered to do his hair.

I jumped to conclusions. "Got some action last night?"

He plopped down in his chair. "No. I just didn't get any sleep."

"Why not?" Cypress asked.

He rested both elbows on the desk before he looked at us. "Amelia called me in tears last night. She called Evan, and he wouldn't give her the time of day. Doesn't want to see the kids. She thinks his new woman is purposely keeping him away."

My palm twitched because I immediately pictured myself bitch-slapping both of them. Evan was a pussy for listening to that psycho bitch, and his whore was just evil. Rose and Lily should the number one priority in his life, not some slut. "Fucking piece of shit."

Cypress clenched his jaw tightly. "I'm seriously gonna break every bone in his body. He obviously doesn't need them judging from the way he spends his free time."

While I was still pissed, I forced myself to focus on what was important. "Is she okay?"

"She was pretty worked up about it," Ace said. "Cried for a while. I talked her down. Reminded her that she has all of us. The girls have Cypress, Blade, and me as father figures. It's not like they're alone."

"True..." I knew Ace said he didn't want anything serious with Amelia, but he definitely bent over backward to be there for her. Not too many people would do that. It made me hope that he would get his head on straight and quit the single life. He would be the man Amelia deserved all along.

"Totally," Cypress said.

"But I'm still gonna confront him," Ace said. "Amelia said she wanted to speak to him on her own. Well, she did that, and it didn't work. So I'm getting involved now."

"Then I am too," Cypress said. "No one treats my nieces like that."

"And my sister," I added. "I'm coming."

Blade walked inside, whistling like he was having a good morning. He stopped when he saw the dead look in Ace's eyes. "Shit, did you sleep on the sidewalk or what?"

Ace shook his head then told him about Evan.

"I say we kill him," Blade said. "Think about it. All of his assets would go to the girls. That's all he has to offer anyway."

"I say we just twist his head on right," Cypress said. "I hate that fucker for what he did to Amelia, but I know the girls need him. Amelia tried talking to him, so I guess we're next."

"Let's not mention this to Amelia," Ace said. "She wouldn't be happy about it."

"No, she wouldn't," I said in agreement. "But Evan might tell her."

"I doubt it," Ace said. "It sounds like they hardly speak to each other. We'll give him the chance to make it work on his own. Maybe that'll help smooth over the tense relationship."

"Maybe," I said in agreement. "So, we'll go after work?"

"Yeah," Ace answered.

Cypress nodded. "I have a feeling I'm going to jail tonight."

"Me too," Blade said.

I watched Amelia walk past the windows as she headed to the door. "Hopefully, the cops put us all in the same cell."

Evan worked in finance in Monterey. Most of his clients lived in Big Sur, Carmel-by-the-Sea, and Pacific Grove. He turned people's fortunes into even bigger fortunes, and as a result, he did pretty well for himself.

That's probably why his mistress had stuck around.

We knew approaching him at the house wasn't a smart move since his whore would be there, so we went to his office just before he left for the day. His black Mercedes was out front, and we walked inside the sleek office with walls that were pregnant with success. His secretary sat in the front in a black skirt and top. She was pretty, and now I wondered if he'd hooked up with her too.

She looked up when she saw all of us. "Mr. Martin is

leaving for the day. I can make you an appointment for this week."

Ace led the charge, standing in front and looking the scariest. "We're gonna see him now."

She stared at us, a little frightened.

"Tell him," he repeated with a quiet voice. "It's Ace." He pointed to Cypress. "Cypress." Then he pointed to me. "Bree." He nodded to Blade. "And Blade. He'll know who we are and what we want to talk about."

Instead of calling his office, she walked down the hallway and disappeared. A few minutes later, she came out. "He'll see you."

"That's what I thought..." Ace said under his breath.

We walked down the hallway and entered Evan's large office. He had two sofas and a big window that overlooked the ocean and the harbor. Seagulls sat on telephone poles and the rooftops of other buildings.

He sat behind his desk, looking calm despite the hostility. He hit the button on his intercom. "Cynthia, you can leave for the day."

No witnesses. Perfect.

"Are you sure?" she said back.

"Yes." He sat back in his chair and looked at us, no longer the handsome man that I remembered. Now he was just a liar. He was evil. He left my sister when someone better came along. I knew exactly how that felt, and I'd never wanted my sister to know that pain. "Wanna take a seat?"

"Not really," Cypress said. "I prefer to break faces while standing."

I shouldn't have been surprised that the situation turned to talk of violence so quickly.

Evan continued to keep his cool. "Amelia sent you here?"

"No," I answered. "She doesn't know anything about this. But she told us about your little phone call."

He felt enough shame to look away.

"I spend a lot of time with your little girls." Ace approached the desk and rested both hands on the surface, infecting Evan's space and making him lean away. "Rose is smart, funny, and adventurous. We were at the beach the other day, and she found a jellyfish on the shore. She grabbed a shovel and dug a trench so the jellyfish could return to the water." He pointed to his temple. "She's got brains. She's gonna be a doctor or a veterinarian or something like that. Lily is sweet. When I cut my finger pulling weeds for Amelia, she cleaned me up and put a bandage on my finger. They love their mother, obey her, and they've got hearts bigger than all of us put together."

Evan held Ace's look, but he didn't seem so tough anymore. He swallowed the lump in his throat and shifted his position.

"Do you realize how lucky you are?" Ace whispered. "Not only did you have a beautiful woman who loved you, but you have two healthy, awesome kids. You keep going down this road, you're gonna lose them. Someone is gonna replace you, and when you're ready to be a father again, they aren't gonna care. So step up and be a man."

"We're always gonna hate you for what you did to Amelia," Cypress added. "You'll never be welcome among us. Not now, not ever. But if you could get your shit together and just be a good father, we can at least be civil to you. Do the right thing, man. Don't do this to your girls."

"Please," I whispered. "Amelia is a strong person, but

she can't replace you. She can't be a mother and a father. Every time the girls ask for you, she doesn't know what to say. You're really gonna let your mistress keep you away from your responsibility?"

"They aren't dogs that you can send to the pound," Blade said. "They're fucking kids."

Ace crossed his arms over his chest. "This is the time for you to decide what kind of man you want to be. Are you the kind of guy who runs off with a whore and abandons his kids? Or are you the guy who's still a father even if he's not a husband?"

Evan sat in silence, not making eye contact with any of us.

Ace leaned forward. "I'm talking to you."

Evan leaned back. "And I heard you."

"What does that mean?" I asked. "Are you gonna pull your head out of your ass and get your shit together?" We agreed we wouldn't raise our voices or drop curse words because it would just escalate the conversation, but I was losing my temper.

"I said I heard you," Evan said. "Of course, I love my girls."

"Then show it, asshole," Ace snapped. "Fucking be there."

Evan nodded.

"Does that mean you're gonna be there?" Cypress asked. "Spend the day with them once a week?"

"I'll try," Evan answered.

"You'll try?" I asked incredulously. "What the fuck does that mean?"

"I will," Evan said. "Now get out of my office."

"You will?" I repeated. "You'll start being a father?"

Evan rose to his feet, dismissing the conversation. "I heard your message, alright? I'm not retarded."

Ace clenched his jaw. "You left Amelia for a woman who doesn't hold a candle to her. If you ask me, you're the biggest dipshit on the planet."

Blade was the only one with a car that could fit five people, so we rode back with him to Carmel. He parked in his garage, and we said our goodbyes before we started walking home. Since Cypress and I were neighbors, we always traveled as a pair.

But I wanted some alone time with Ace.

"Cypress, I want to walk with Ace alone for a little bit."

Cypress eyed the both of us, not with jealousy but suspicion. "Okay."

"I'll catch up with you."

He eyed both of us again before he turned away and took a different road that led to Casanova.

Ace walked toward his house without stopping, his hands in the pockets of his jacket. Night was settling on the city, and pretty soon it would be dark. "What's up?"

"For a guy who doesn't have feelings for my sister, you're certainly invested in her life."

He stared straight ahead, his large physique shifting as he moved. "She's my friend. Of course, I'm invested."

"You're a lot more invested than Cypress, and he's her brother-in-law." Now I was beginning to say things like that out loud, that Cypress really was my husband and we were family, even if I didn't remember how we got there.

"Whether we're related by blood, marriage, or nothing at all, she's family. I'd do the same for you."

"We both know I wouldn't call you in the middle of the night crying. Come on, be real with me."

He stared straight ahead.

"I think you have feelings for her."

Still, nothing.

"I just don't know why you don't want to be with her. Doesn't add up."

"I like playing the field. I like being single. I like fucking who I want to fuck without explanation."

I believed that—but not entirely. "Then why are you spending so much time with Rose and Lily? Why do you always walk Amelia home? Why are you the first person she calls when she needs something? I used to be that person."

"Maybe because I'm a gentleman."

"You just said you want to fuck anyone and everyone. By that logic, you aren't a gentleman. Something about Amelia makes you different."

He shook his head with a slight smile on his lips. "You're a pain in the ass, you know that?"

"Yep. You aren't the first person to tell me that."

He stopped walking and turned to me. The sun was officially gone, and all the refracted beams of light lit the small town. I'd have to use the flashlight on my phone to make it the rest of the way back. His pretty eyes weren't so friendly anymore. Now he looked irritated. "Bree, what do you want?"

"I want to know why you don't want to be with Amelia. And I want the real reason. No bullshit about wanting to sleep around. No lies about not wanting to be a stepdad. I see the way you look at Amelia and the girls. You can't fool me."

He shifted his weight then looked down the street, like

Cypress or Blade would appear out of nowhere. "You want the truth, huh?"

My heart pounded in my chest. "I'm not leaving you alone until I get it."

"I'm not gonna tell you unless you promise to keep it to yourself."

"Why can't I tell Amelia?"

"Because you can't," he said. "And if you break your word, I'll never trust you again. Do you understand?"

I needed Ace's trust, as friends and business partners.

"Are you sure you want to know? It'd be easier just to move on and not stick your nose where it doesn't belong."

"She's my sister. I'll always stick my nose in her business. Now tell me."

"Then you're giving me your word?"

After Cypress broke my trust, I never wanted to break anyone else's. I knew what it was like to be deceived. It hurt—a lot. "I give you my word."

"Alright. Yeah, I have feelings for her. Ever since she told me how she felt, I haven't stopped thinking about it. Instead of fucking Lady or whoever, I spend my time wishing I were with Amelia. But I know…eventually… Evan is gonna come back. And when he does, she'll choose him over me. I would never recover from that."

I tilted my head to the side, surprised this was the obstacle keeping them apart. "Ace, you have no idea what she would do."

"She would pick him," he repeated. "And since he's the father of her kids, she should. If they have any chance to be a family again, they have to try."

"Not after what he did to her."

He shrugged. "When he wakes up, he's gonna realize he made the biggest mistake of his life. I know he will.

Amelia isn't just some woman. She's unbelievable. When the novelty wears off with this other woman, he'll realize he had something amazing with Amelia. He won't stop until he gets her back."

"Ace, she'd never take him back."

He didn't repeat himself. "Even if she didn't, I don't want to be the reason they aren't a family."

"Even if you weren't her boyfriend, she still wouldn't take him back. I know her."

"And I know her better. I know how much she loved him. I know how hurt she was when he left. I was there, Bree. You weren't."

I took a deep breath when the hit sank into me.

"I'm sorry," he whispered. "I can't let myself fall in love with her. If she broke my heart, I'd never get back on my feet. I've already fallen hard for Rose and Lily. If I had to pack my stuff and leave them...that would hurt even more."

Hearing all these sweet things made my eyes wet. I wished my sister had never married Evan. I wished Ace had told her how he felt well before she married someone else. He was the person she should be with, not Evan. "Ace, you have to try. You're making your decision based on events that may never happen. Maybe Evan marries this woman and never tries to get back together with Amelia. You have no idea."

"Instinct is a pretty powerful thing, Bree."

"I think this is a mistake. I think she should be with you, Ace. And I would tell her that if she ever asked."

"Well, if you keep your word, you never should," he said. "I trust you, Bree. Don't give me a reason not to."

Now I was stuck at a crossroads, debating whether I should tell my sister or not. But Ace was one of my closest friends. I didn't want to lose his confidence as well as his respect. "I sincerely hope you think it over. Because I believe you're wrong."

Cypress was sitting on the stairs in front of his door with Dino beside him, obviously waiting for me to walk home.

"You didn't need to wait up for me."

Dino ran to me with his tongue hanging out.

I couldn't resist that face no matter how hard I tried. I kneeled down and petted him, letting him lick me across the cheek a few times. "Hey, Dino. Thanks for waiting up for me."

"So you thank him but not me?" Cypress asked as he stood up.

"He's a guard dog."

"And I'm a guard husband." He walked toward me with his hands in the pockets of his jeans.

I stood up and looked into Cypress's face, seeing the handsome and stern expression he wore.

"What did you talk about with Ace?"

I couldn't say. "Just stuff about Amelia."

"Like?"

"I asked if he had feelings for her because it seems like he does."

"And what did he say?"

I felt bad for lying, but I had to keep my promise. "Said he didn't."

"He said the same to me. I think he sees her as a sister, the way I see her too."

Ace definitely didn't see her like a sister. Cypress was totally blind. "Yeah..."

Cypress moved in closer to me, his shadow approaching mine. His face was visible, but the street was dark and most things were indistinguishable. His hands slid around my waist, and he came close to me, close enough for a kiss.

I knew where this was going. "Not tonight." If I let it happen too many times, my logic would become blurred.

"I just want to hold you." He pressed his forehead to mine and brought me close to him. "I love sex as much as the next guy, but there's nothing better in life than holding the woman you love." He closed his eyes and tightened his grip on me.

I'd have to be made of stone for those words not to sink into my heart. My hands slid up his arms, feeling the bulge of his biceps under his shirt. His cologne washed over me, reminding me of the smell of his bedroom. I closed my eyes and cherished the closeness, unable to resist how good it felt.

The night deepened, and the three of us stood there together. I didn't want to go inside and sleep even though I was exhausted. I didn't even think about what Ace told me about Amelia. I just thought about the man in front of me, the man I'd promised to love until the day I died.

I didn't trust him.

But I still felt just as strongly for him as I did when I first laid eyes on him. My heart reacted anytime he was near. When he said the right words, I melted at his feet. I couldn't resist his charm or his sincerity.

I suspected I knew how this was going to end.

And there was nothing I could do to stop it.

I moved my head until my mouth brushed against his. I gave him a light kiss, feeling the stubble from his chin rub against my soft skin. As if the world went quiet just for us, I enjoyed the sensation, the burn of our mouths once they touched. I felt the jolt of passion, of sensual desperation.

I felt everything.

He kissed me back, keeping it slow and gentle. His lips met mine with purposeful kisses. His tongue never came into contact with mine, but it was still one of the sexiest kisses we'd shared. It wasn't based on lust, but something a lot deeper.

I pulled my mouth away when the kiss went on longer than it should. The affection went to my head, my heart, and everywhere else. "Good night…"

He kept his grip on me, refusing to let me go. He looked me in the eye, his intensity stronger than it'd ever been before. "I believe in us. And I'll never stop believing."

ALSO BY E. L. TODD

The story continues in 325 First Fights

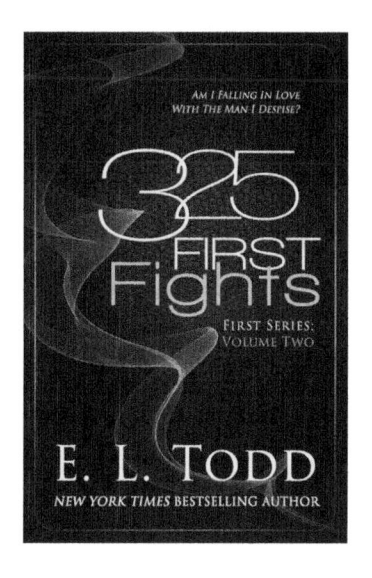

Order Now

AFTERWORD

Dear Reader,

Thank you for reading 400 First Kisses. I hope you enjoyed reading it as much as I enjoyed writing it. If you could leave a short review, it would help me so much! Those reviews are the best kind of support you can give an author. Thank you!

Wishing you love,

E. L. Todd

WANT TO STALK ME?

Subscribe to my newsletter for updates on new releases, giveaways, and for my comical monthly newsletter. You'll get all the dirt you need to know. Sign up today.

www.eltoddbooks.com

Facebook:
https://www.facebook.com/ELTodd42

Twitter:
@E_L_Todd

Now you have no reason not to stalk me. You better get on that.

EL'S ELITES

I know I'm lucky enough to have super fans, you know, the kind that would dive off a cliff for you. They have my back through and through. They love my books, and they love spreading the word. Their biggest goal is to see me on the New York Times bestsellers list, and they'll stop at nothing to make it happen. While it's a lot of work, it's also a lot of fun. What better way to make friendships than to connect with people who love the same thing you do?

Are you one of these super fans?

If so, send a request to join the Facebook group. It's closed, so you'll have a hard time finding it without the link. Here it is:

https://www.facebook.com/groups/1192326920784373

Hope to see you there, ELITE!

Printed in Great Britain
by Amazon